# The Path

# By Richard M Pearson

Richard M Pearson released his first novel 'The Path' at the ripe old age of 58. I grew up in England, Wales, Northern Ireland and then finally Scotland. I have always loved reading and books that build up a gothic atmosphere have continued to fire my imagination, Dracula being a classic example.

A few years ago I did a week-long walk across the spectacular Galloway hills of Scotland and inspired by their incredible beauty and solitude I decided to pen my first book. Now I am retired I intend to continue my literary journey. I hope my book will inspire more people to visit that lonely part of Scotland, maybe you will even meet the ghost of the forest.

Dedicated to Maureen, Karen and Lauren.

# Table of Contents

The path waited for us as it always had. The dead winter leaves sinking into the bog pinned down by cold cruel rain. Nothing had come this way all year, maybe nothing had ever come this way. The trees listened silent and tall, the water trickled and spread over the rocks searching for our footsteps, the mist hung in the air watching over the little valley. They had waited an eternity for the day we would finally arrive. And now at long last, they could sense the moment was coming and the black mass of the forest could get ready to take its revenge.

# Prologue

I know it might be a million to one shot but if by any chance you live in the town of Chelmsford could I ask you to do me one last little favour? I am going to assume one of you might say yes so thanks for that, it really does mean a lot to me. If you find St John's road and walk up to the end where it makes a T junction with Moulsham Drive could you then please turn right. About fifty yards down the road you will see a red post box, you can't miss it as it's also got two friends standing beside it, a grey metal box on a post and a green box cemented onto the pavement. I have no idea what the last two are for but to be honest it doesn't really matter. What I need you to do is turn around directly in front of the green box and look at the red brick wall facing you, yes that's the one. Now look down and lying on the pavement against the wall will be an old discarded copy of the Chelmsford and Mid Essex Times. It's one of those free local papers that come out every week, you know the kind that has headlines like, *Chelmsford voted eighth best place to live in Essex* or *Local grandmother gives birth to triplets.* Anyway, I digress. What I really want you to do is pick up the newspaper if it's not too soggy or dirty and turn to page five. Can you see a small paragraph about halfway down the page? The headline should say something like,

1

*Body of missing Chelmsford man found in remote Scottish Loch.*

Yes, that's it; you have it now, would you be so kind and read it for me? That's brilliant; you really have been a star, thanks ever so much. Unfortunately, I suppose I am going to have to assume that most of you don't live in Chelmsford though so here is a transcript of what the little article says underneath the headline.

*Chelmsford Police today confirmed that the body pulled out from Loch Dee in a remote part of Galloway, Scotland was that of missing sixty-two-year-old Chelmsford man Ralph Casalles. Mr. Casalles was believed to have been living in homeless shelters for a number of years having suffered from alcohol-related health problems. Meghan Casalles, his estranged wife, had reported him missing when friends and family members mentioned that they had not seen him around for several months.*

Look I know it's not exactly tabloid fame and only amounts to a few words in a free newspaper, but it was nice of them to at least make the effort. I realise the bit about me was sort of hidden between the story about the church fete and the missing cat, but it did make me feel important for a second or so. Maybe not quite the fifteen minutes of fame Andy Warhol once promised everybody but hey, how many of you will get a mention in the local press when the grim reaper comes calling? I wanted to smile when I read it but then thought it might be considered as bad taste, I don't think the living tend to see the dead as the jovial kind. We are sort of expected to mope around in dark corners with bits of flesh hanging off our corpses while trying to scare the shit out of everyone, I suppose.

## Memorial

This stone is not who I was

This tomb is not what I became

Remember me not for this cold rock

But see me as one who loved and lived and smiled

This heart once beat like yours

This shadow once followed the sun

Think of me as you walk by to tend to your recent dead

And leave me one last flower to show that I am not

forgotten

# 1- Nine Fifteen

"Meg I can't find the spare front door key." Jeez, why does everything seem to get so much harder as you get older? Last night I had checked over my bag, shoes, clothes, money for the hundredth time, more with anticipation and excitement than any real worry that anything had changed from audit number ninety-nine performed only a few hours before. I was at the age where you had to double check everything and then double check it all again. It was the only way to be sure that your memory would not play tricks on you. I had already started to put dirty washing in the bin rather than the wash basket, tea bags into the fridge rather than the cupboard and losing my phone was a daily if not hourly occurrence. Often it would turn up in the oddest places, once it had even rung out from the bin to be found mixed in with old food and my dirty washing. Meg would comment in sympathetic tones, "Everyone in their late fifties loses things; it's not dementia Ralph it's because you don't concentrate." She did have a point I suppose, I could still recount endless football and music facts from years ago with ease while searching the bin for my phone or the fridge for tea bags.

"Have you got your keys, money, walking shoes, head?" Meg was trying to inject some humour as we kissed at the front door, the way she always did when I started to get stressed and lose my temper. It played on my mind that she seemed so cheerful; surely it was her duty to at least pretend to be sad that I was going to be out of her life for a week. In reality, I knew she was looking forward to time alone without me, no one to moan about the endless chats on the phone with family and friends or about spending too much money on things we already had. A week of not having to help search for my keys or phone, a week of not having to tell me every evening that I was drinking too much. "Ralph do you really need to open another bottle, its eleven o'clock, you know you will feel like shit in the morning and regret it." The words would be followed by an angry exchange and usually end with Meg heading off in a strop to bed while I tried to find the bottle opener. No doubt it would be in the fridge or the bin at this point along with my phone.

Surely every couple went through difficulties after twenty-six years together, even more so once the children left home and you had nothing to deflect your attention, just the two of you trying to make it work. That was the problem though, it was not two just the two of us. I loved alcohol more than my wife, drink was now my mistress and I would take every opportunity to indulge her. It had been a gradual romance that had not really taken off until I reached my mid-thirties, now twenty years later it was a full-grown affair. I did not even try to hide my lover from Meg anymore; she lived with us now and more often than not joined me in the spare room if I had been exiled for the night. It was one of those things in life that you hated yourself for doing but still did it anyway. I suppose they would call me a functioning alcoholic, one who could hold down a job, still just about keep a marriage together and even put the bins out every week. When I was a child growing up in the sixties and seventies every adult I knew would have fitted the category of functioning alcoholic including my parents. Nowadays it had become stigmatised, endless articles in the newspaper about how many units you could have each week before your liver gave you a month's notice that it was packing up and calling it a day. Countless celebrities on daytime television show's making you feel even guiltier, *I used to drink one glass of wine every day, it was awful; I knew I had reached rock bottom when I started to pour that second glass. I finally quit in 2016 and now I feel so much better.*

I had played this moment over in my head for years now. The point where I would finally have the courage to break the pattern and walk out of the front door without it being part of someone else's scheme, someone else's strategy for my life. This was it, I was finally heading to the wilds of Southern Scotland for a week, without any real plan other than a rough idea to walk 20 miles a day and sleep in hillside camping huts. More than fifty years of domestication was strangling me, the fingers of suburbia gripped around my

7

throat, an endless routine of work and home life, an endless repetition of trying to fit in and please the same people over and over again. I hoped that the chance to clear my head and start again would recharge my batteries, maybe it was naive, but I dreamed of returning as a new man, happy and ready to embrace how lucky I was in life. Most of the time it felt as though the world was happening while I simply watched from a distance as if it was nothing to do with me? It was not as though I did not have a good job, I seemed to be respected as a project manager after more than twenty years at Creswell Avionics, Christ I had got further than I ever expected to, further than I felt I deserved. And yet Instead of feeling a success, I felt like a fraud, guilty for having a good job, a marriage that had survived despite my shortcomings and kids who had made the progression into adulthood far more smoothly than I had ever done.

Even my friends had negotiated the midlife crisis better than me. While I floundered about looking for the spark that would ignite my passion again, they had charged headfirst into their bucket list to become either lycra-clad cyclists or pot-bellied hells angels on their shiny big Japanese motorbikes. Even the new woman and three times married gang seemed to keep their home run going, "Hi Ralph, have you met Helga before?"

While I am thinking to myself, "What the fuck happened to Julia?"

I could always find a reason not to throw myself into something that would change the pattern. Too costly, too risky, no I am past the age to do that, and so on. There was always a negative to keep the positive at bay, always a door closed against change. I knew, in reality, I had just become lazy, too comfortable doing the same thing week after week, too happy to sit each night slowly drifting into an alcohol-induced slumber. This was my chance, maybe my last chance to start the change and make life exciting again; well that's what I told myself at least. Deep down I knew the real reason as I held Meg tightly in a farewell embrace that morning and she did too. I was hoping my going would break the chain and leave the demon behind, the one that sat beside me forever gaining strength, gradually taking control to eventually own me. I had to stop drinking before it was too late. It was decision time; if I came back from my expedition still hand in hand with the mistress then my marriage was over.

Harvey was the odd guy at work, not odd as in weird as he was friendly enough, but he always seemed peripheral to every clique or group in the office. Constantly ready to crack a joke or comment but never asked to share a table at the canteen unless it was by accident. *Fuck here comes that fruit loop Harvey, just get a table for four so he can't join us.* Thinking about it

I knew why, it was timing, too quick to jump in and show he was an expert, always ready to give an opinion when it was not asked for. Too eager to please people with a witty remark in the hope he could break into the circle and become part of the club. You can't do that in the office political system, you must know your place and understand that it takes years of graft to move up the workplace social order. Sod all to do with your actual job, you could be the vice president and still be the fifth one to arrive at a four-person table. It was not that he was a dislikeable; he just seemed to remind me of a puppy desperate for affection, as though he had *please be my friend* stamped on his forehead. Don't ask me how but for some reason this oddball had ended up being my walking companion, my shadow for a week as we headed off into the unknown side by side. I had initially planned to go by myself, but Meg made it easy for me, "You can't do that alone, what if you break a leg and no one is there to help you." It had not been hard to abdicate because I was a coward and wanted to be talked out of a solo trip. I had not chosen Harvey to accompany me of course; somehow it just seemed to happen while I watched like a detached observer. At the time I had put it down to just being another example of his lousy understanding of the office hierarchy system, now looking back I know he chose me and from that point on my fate was sealed.

I turned at the end of the street and looked back at the detached house that had been our home for nearly thirty years. The paint looked faded after the slaughter of winter, the tangled bushes in the garden surrounded by dead sodden leaves. The weather-stained slabs on the drive and path cried out for that sparkle of life again that only the footprints of children could bring. It had once looked fresh and exciting, part of our family, part of us. Now it seemed ready for modern blood, the challenge of the new, make over time. If it could speak it was telling me it was almost time to go, time to hand over the keys to the next wide-eyed couple, the enthusiastic young man who planned to take on the world and the heavily pregnant young woman who held his arm tightly and radiated the future. It was time to renew the cycle, the rollercoaster was slowing down as it came around to its starting point again and soon the door would open to allow me and Meg to finally walk away.

It was a cold but bright early March morning as I swung around and continued to walk down Manor Road. One of those days when you can feel spring's renewal in the air as it fights to spread its infant seeds over the decaying blanket of winter. I had decided to do the trek early in the year before flies and midges invaded the Galloway forests and made things unbearable. The trade-off would be the weather but freezing to death sounded marginally less painful than being eaten alive. To be honest I was not too keen on any kind of crawly things, probably not the best attribute for an explorer I suppose. I could imagine scraping through to the final two for Christopher Columbus's next expedition, "Mr. Casalles I can't make my mind up as you both gave such good interviews. Is there anything you want to say that could convince me why I should choose you rather than the other candidate, Sir Ranulph Fiennes?"

"Right ok, let me think about this one. Yes, I do have one last question. Will there be any spiders around when we reach the new world?"

Like an automaton I had completed this same walk to the office near Chelmsford station every day for the last twenty-five years, often arriving thirty minutes later without any memory of the actual journey. Today was different, I felt ridiculously self-conscious, dressed in conspicuously new walking gear as well as carrying an overloaded rucksack on my back. Of course, I had been on a few practise walks but always went to the starting point by car and timed things to make sure the exercise went mostly unseen. This morning I was mixing with the late commuters, school kids, shoppers, feeling like an alien and looking like one as well. It would be good to meet Harvey at the station and then the embarrassment could at least be shared. I felt excitement at the prospect of being away from everything for a week but had an unusual sense of trepidation as well. I knew why, it was not the twenty miles a day over hills and bogs; it was spending a week with a stranger, another man in fact. I was going to have to share my personal space with someone I hardly knew, let another human being see the real me, the one only Meg got close to these days. The thoughts made me feel guilty for feeling slightly homophobic. I had been away with male groups before but that was the problem, groups made it feel safer. Meg had teased me about sharing space with another man and as usual, I snapped at her for what had been a bit of fun, but I knew in my mind that it needled me because I was stepping out of my comfort zone.

Totally forgetting I was dressed like a Martian I struggled into Shaheed's shop to get a coffee from the machine, something I did every morning as a reward for making the effort to get out of bed and go to work. By the time I realised, it was too late to back out. Any attempt to turn around would have sent the neatly stacked tins of Spam or green toothbrushes crashing to the floor. The other option was to take the bloody rucksack off but that was a nonstarter, it had taken ten minutes this morning to attach it to my back and that was with Meg helping me. "Are you heading off to climb the Himalayas today?" Saheed commented in his usual monotonous bored tone but other than that not a single question regarding the reason for my attire. I could have walked in dressed as an Eskimo and still Saheed would have kept the conversation going the same way he did with me every morning. *This weather is awful, the roads are so busy, but no one ever stops at the small shops, the supermarkets are killing us, how can we compete on price.*

*Maybe it's because you are a robbing greedy bastard,* I wanted to reply but then decided not to as I really wanted that coffee. It had always irked me that Saheed had the audacity to charge more than a pound for one of those chocolate bars that already cost a ridiculous eighty pence everywhere else despite being half the size they had been in the seventies. I tried to inject some of the excitement I felt about the upcoming trek into the conversation, but the effort proved to be pointless as it was obvious he was not listening. Saheed was already formulating his next complaint while waiting impatiently for me to shut up, "You at least get a holiday, if I closed the shop even for one day it would never re-open again, we just can't compete with the big shops anymore." His small stooped frame handed over my change and then turned dismissively to focus on whatever he had been doing before I walked in.

My ego felt dented twice already, first Meg and now the ever-optimistic Saheed, did they not realise I was marching into the unknown to face potentially life-threatening danger? I watched the coffee dispenser for the millionth time as it went through the usual morning ritual, a shot of coffee then water and a final flourish as it hissed out steam and hot milk. The last part always made me jump and step back, I don't know why as I knew what was coming but it felt rude not to acknowledge its daily effort to force me out of my morning coma. Sometimes I felt closer to the coffee machine than I did to most human beings; at least it did its job without complaining. I grabbed my plastic cup and left feeling deflated but comfortable in the knowledge that Saheed's shop would always be around selling coffee and overpriced chocolate bars despite the march of the supermarket.

The weather seemed to change, becoming colder and darker as I walked the last half mile to the railway station. It was that sudden dimming of the light that precedes a snow flurry, I prayed not. I thought about Harvey and tried to piece together what I knew about him. Far taller than me but that would not be difficult, single and never been married but with a long-term girlfriend. It was hard not to view the never married bit without a hint of suspicion although of course in this age of political correctness I knew it was wrong to think that way. But come on, let's be honest, we all think it. If someone says they have never been married, then it's hard not to wonder what is wrong with them. It's the same if someone tells you they have been divorced four times, if it's a man we automatically put them down as a wife beater and if it's a woman then she must be a money grabber, and probably has at least one ex-husband buried under the slabs in the back garden. Having a girlfriend conjured up the image of a sexual relationship and surely that was something young people did not fifty-six-year-old men with our protruding stomachs and thinning hair. The thought of Harvey having sex with his girlfriend was almost as bad as having the knowledge that my parents must have had sex together at least once in their lives. It must have been the one day my parents ran out of booze and the shops had closed. "Mrs. Casalles I am afraid we have run out of gin and as its 1959 as well as being the Sabbath then the shops will be shut until Monday." Ok Mr. Casalles, well shall we have our one and only sexual encounter and make Ralph until we can restock the gin supply tomorrow?"

Harvey had only been with the company for six months as a freelance contractor having recently moved to Chelmsford from the nearby city of Norwich. I had interacted with him a few times as part of a project team at work but thinking back it was difficult to pin down any real contribution he made other than to talk and play for the laughs. Having spent most of his life moving around the country working on short-term contracts he had developed that who cares attitude I found prevalent in most temporary employees i.e. *who gives a fuck? When it all goes pear shaped I will be out of here anyway and onto my next job.* Harvey was one of that rare breed of business people who never replied to texts or emails or if he did it would be two days after you needed the response and then it no longer mattered. How did guys like him survive? I guess that was it really, by never committing to anything or taking individual responsibility then he could never be blamed when things went wrong. A presence rather than an entity, someone you remembered but never really considered. Of course, he still contributed but somehow Harvey always managed to agree with an idea rather than coming up with one. I suppose in a way I really envied him, probably earned more than I did without any of the stress. He had worked out exactly how to play the game for maximum return and minimum effort, it was me who was the real fool, he just played the fool. Almost at the station, time to clear these thoughts and let the voices in my head have a rest. Try to look calm, excited and ready to face the great expedition together, jeez poor Harvey, condemned before we had even said good morning just because I was jealous that he still had sex in his late fifties.

Platform one for the train to London, for once not jam-packed with commuters or shoppers. A sharp cold wind is blowing targeting the platform, looking for me. Tickets all booked, Harvey of course was the more experienced expedition expert, knew the route, had walked in Scotland before, well at least that's what he kept telling me. It had been his choice; the South of Scotland is mostly bypassed by tourists heading to the Highlands and walkers attempting the more popular West Highland Way. For us, it was the rarely

17

used and remote Southern Upland path from Dalgowan to Stranraer on the coast. A trek of nearly one hundred miles ending beside a forgotten edge of Scotland that faced out to The Irish Sea.

Listening to Harvey's exultations on how remote this part of the country could be and how beautiful it was had made it sound like the perfect choice for our trek. Of course, like all true project managers I had completed some intensive research to make sure I could hold my own as well as trying to work on my fitness if not the drinking. I felt ready for the challenge but was also scared shitless at the thought of collapsing after five miles, screaming to go home and then having to face the rest of my office life being sent to the periphery. Demoted down the pecking order while Harvey proudly held court telling everyone how he had carried me on his shoulders back to the station, tears of failure running down my face while he calmly lit a cigarette and stood nonchalantly staring into the distance like Cary Grant. No doubt the rest of my career would entail being the fifth person to arrive at the four-seat table. *Shit, clear your fucking head Ralph you are away again*. He is there standing in front of the platform coffee kiosk reading a map, looking like a seasoned walker with his rucksack and woollen hat covering the top of his balding head while still allowing unreasonably long white curls to flow out of the sides, nothing like Cary Grant in fact. Maybe I can tell him, *no need for the map yet, you just board the fucking train and get off in London*, even I can do that bit without a guidebook.

We both try to speak first but I beat him to it. "Good morning old chap, well this is it just two trains and we arrive in remote Scotland at long last."

"Two!" replies Harvey in an overemphasised tone of surprise "Why two?"

Already my defences are up as I know I have already given ground in the race to become expedition leader. I try to fumble my way out of it while waiting for the inevitable humiliation of being corrected within 30 seconds of meeting up.

"Its three trains", continues Harvey like a school teacher scolding his pupil for not doing their homework properly." Here to London, Virgin Pendelino from London to Carlisle then change to the local train for Dalgowan."

"Oh, I thought the train from London was direct to Dalgowan," I retorted while feeling my cheeks start to go red.

"Hahaha, it's well seeing you have never been to Scotland Ralph old chap, Virgin express trains don't run directly to places like Dalgowan, they only recently discovered electricity for fuck sake." Not only had I been humbled but a nagging thought was forming in my head, Harvey was a train spotter and any minute now he would pull out his notebook and start to tell me the actual numbers of the trains we would be getting. *So that's why he had never been married.* I patted him sympathetically on the shoulder while working on my reply.

"Well thank goodness you are with me; I could have ended up in Wales." My abdication and attempt at humour helped to break the ice and put us back on equal terms for now at least.

The cold wind swirled up as the train pulled into the platform. The weather forecast was not good and already I was concerned that if it was this cold in the South then what would it be like 400 miles further North. We made it to London and rather than dragging the rucksacks on the underground we hailed a taxi to get to us to Euston from Liverpool Street station. "Are you two boys off camping then? A bit early in the year for me," came the weird but friendly electronic voice from the speaker in the back of the cab.

"Oh, are you a hill walker as well then?" I replied to the driver trying to come across as though I was Sir Edmund Hillary.

"Nah, never walked a hill in my life mate, furthest I walk is to the pub on a Friday," came the reply that firmly put me in my place. And as if I did not already feel like an idiot Harvey chipped in with, "You and Ralph should get together, he has never climbed any hills either," followed by a friendly nudge in the ribs.

We arrived at Euston having already blown half our budget on a black cab and boarded the big Virgin thing Harvey had mentioned. I noted with relief that he neither took down the train number nor showed any slight interest in our mode of transport. When leaving the taxi, he had headed straight over to an off-licence though and arrived back with three bottles of wine and a big grin. "These little beauties will do until we get to the pub tonight and have a real drink Ralph old chap." Maybe old guys with girlfriends were not so bad after all I thought to myself. Scrambling into the carriage I felt the relief as the rucksack was removed from my back, already I hated it and we had not left London yet. We made light conversation for a while without really saying anything, I thought about Meg, was she missing me, or had she even noticed I was gone? Or even worse, maybe she was celebrating my departure and the thought of freedom while dancing naked around the house with a glass of wine as one of those god-awful lounge singers she liked blared out from the speakers. When I left home on business trips I always seemed to miss her but on returning I could never put those feelings into words or actions. Why could I not be that handsome but mysterious all-around human being I longed to be but somehow always ended up being short-tempered and then annoyed with myself for failing to reach the dreamed of standards I set myself. I wanted to whisk her off to a posh restaurant or one of those nightclubs where bow-tied James Bond lookalikes played the grand piano while couples waltzed around the floor. The reality was I would sink into the armchair with a glass in my hand while thinking, *maybe tomorrow*.

Staring out of the window I could see London suburbia flash past followed by a gradual change to imposing scattered red brick houses with big manicured gardens. No doubt the large double garages would each hold a him and her Range Rover as well as a sit on lawn mower. Some of the mansions still had lights shining from the occasional room like a lighthouse beacon glowing through the dim winter morning. I wondered what all these people did, had they all found the meaning of life or was it just me who was fucked up. Probably not, but the individual buildings seemed to have a radiance that ours lacked, maybe it was the occupants who gave the house its spirit and mine had seeped away year by year until I barely existed.

The scenery started to change after a few hours and the saying *it's grim up north* came to mind, not helped by the mist and dampness that seemed to pervade the fields and scattered villages as they flashed by. I had started to drowse as we pulled into Preston, the name made me feel like an explorer on the way to uncharted territories or maybe it was just the wine kicking in. The seats opposite had *booked from Preston* showing on the tiny screen at the side of them. Our small talk had included the usual man patter of *let's hope it is two hot looking women that have reserved, and they are walking the Southern Upland Way*. We did not go as far as lewd pub talk would though, no doubt that would come; it always did with male relationships. For now, we kept it clean until we understood the boundaries and got to know each other. Strangely it was an older man who boarded and took the seats, but he was alone. You could tell he was a gentleman of the old school, very well spoken, travelling to Scotland to stay with family. He looked tired and careworn as though life had drained out of him and what was left was just biding its time until the inevitable end. Harvey was a talker but one of those people who would initially arouse the interest of strangers in a conversation but soon you could see them becoming bored because he was exactly that, a talker not a listener. The sort of person who you know is already working on their next statement desperately waiting for you to finish whatever you are saying.

I started to drowse and left him to it, the words drifting over me as I fell into one of those uncomfortable periods of sleep where just as you drift off your head bobs down and half wakes you then you go through the whole process again for another five minutes, bob, half wake, bob, half wake. You know that people are smirking to themselves but the need to sleep is overwhelming, so you accept the embarrassment of being a nodding donkey. I heard snippets of talk from the old man more clearly than anything Harvey said but that's because even in my half sleep what he was saying was more interesting and my senses homed in on his words as they faded away. In the twilight world of my dream, I could see the old man's face, deep lines crossing over even deeper lines, every one of them carved as if by a sculptor, each one etched in his skin to tell their own sad story. But it was his eyes that pierced vividly through the dream. Cold dark cruel eyes filled with a hatred that spoke of retribution and revenge.

A jolt followed by the sudden slowing of the train woke me sharply. Harvey was prodding me, that few seconds of drooling confusion when you awake in strange circumstances and your brain must re-sort and re-evaluate exactly where you are and why. "We are slowing for Carlisle, need to get moving Ralphy boy, we only have ten minutes to make the last train of the evening that stops at Dalgowan."

*Who on earth was Ralphy boy!* Any minute now I expected him to start calling me Bunny or some other pet name. I noticed the three bottles of wine were empty on the table though so that probably explained things. The seats opposite was vacant again. "What happened to your mate," I asked.

"Eh, who? They must have gone to the buffet car," he replied in an odd tone.

24

*They*! His answer confused me, but I was already confused and feeling too irritable to follow up with any more questions. My mouth felt dry from the sleep and I longed for another drink. I took a mouthful from my water bottle and wished it was something else.

We stepped out into the faded grandeur of Carlisle Citadel station, almost like a shrunken version of Paddington before it was modernised and turned into a shopping complex with the occasional train standing apologetically in a corner. The station had one of those vast glass roofs that added to its Gothic charm aided even more so by the clatter of wind and rain bouncing off the glass and burrowing through any available gaps to deposit pools of ice cold water onto the few people below. We headed to a side platform where a two-carriage train sat half exposed to the elements, rain running down its windows. The rucksack was already proving to be the enemy, rather than put it back on to take it off again I carried it and internally wept at the thought of the weight and the rain and the cold. I called Meg before boarding to give her an update on our arrival at base camp. Already I felt lonely and all we had done was a train journey. But then wasn't I lonely even in Chelmsford back home, even when Meg was around, even when I was at work, what the hell was wrong with me? Why did it always seem to feel as though I was the only person left in the world? The vast and mostly empty mid-afternoon Carlisle station added to the feeling of isolation, that and the fact I was with someone I was yet to know. I finished talking to Meg and took a last glance at the vista of the station before boarding the carriage. In the distance, a handful of travellers and station staff could be seen shivering in the damp gloom. At the far end of the platform stood the vaguely familiar shape of an old man with a large black dog beside him. Even though it was difficult to make out his face I somehow knew he was looking towards me, staring directly at me. It was as though I could feel his eyes burning deep into my soul.

## Nine Fifteen

It's not the disappointment that kills you, it's the expectation

9.05 sip your coffee slowly, don't look desperate, maybe this will be the day

Coats, hats, Travel cases, people, all moving all with a purpose, all with a destination

Recorded station announcements that no one hears

Raindrops drip through the broken glass roof; even they have a platform to go to

9.08 look at the arrivals board again, the 9:15 on time, same platform as always

Pigeons scavenge, cigarette ends dropped, newspaper vendor, all belong except me

Can this be the day, will this be my day, it's 9:12 time to move, time to believe

Walk slowly, look loved, look like you belong, don't let them see

Platform seven, 9:15, the maroon carriages empty their humanity, empty their life

This time surely, this time you will be here, this time our eyes will meet

The heads are already thinning out, no wave, no rush to embrace; only passing faces

Left to stand on an empty platform with the raindrops with the cigarette ends without you

It's not the disappointment that kills you, it's the expectation

Walk away, an eternity of hours, today is gone but tomorrow will again be 9:15

## 2- Car Graveyard

We stepped off the small train at Dalgowan station to be greeted by a biting wind blowing down from the low moorland hills. The late March rain swirled around us to add to the shock of having just enjoyed hours of warmth and rest. The diesel engines on the sprinter roared in protest as it kicked its way out of the remote station to continue the winding journey through the borders to finish in distant Glasgow. Even the name "Glasgow" conjured up romantic images of shipbuilding, hardship, the notorious razor gangs and street urchins playing football. The reality was no doubt glass-covered office towers, traffic jams and small shops selling overpriced chocolate bars. Just like every other city I suppose.

I heard the words, "let's get booked into the goddam Bed and Breakfast as quickly as possible, I need a fucking drink," penetrate through the driving rain and my tightly zipped coat hood. We had only walked a hundred yards and already I had a feeling that Harvey might not be the cream of the hillwalking crop. Over the preceding months I had tried to convince at least one of my pub drinking friends to join me on the trip and as the evening progressed and the beer flowed I had been swamped with volunteers all talking over each other about what equipment would be needed or over-enthusiastic comments such as, *let's all meet tomorrow and get into training.* This ritual had been repeated over successive weekends only to be followed by silence the next day or maybe a text from someone who had really got carried away, *sorry Ralph, too much beer last night, Rhona would go apeshit if I said I was going walking for a week with the boys. Good luck with the expedition; maybe one of the other guys.* It was hard to even remember how initially Harvey had invited himself along but the one thing that cemented his position had been his willingness to study maps of Southern Scotland and drink beer after work in Chelmsford. To be honest, I did not give a damn whether my companion was fit or had any walking experience; the overriding factor was the person must like alcohol. I was happy to kill myself walking hour after hour so long as it finished with a drink. I needed a like-minded companion because I found it impossible to drink alone without feeling guilty. If someone else did it and even better, drank more than me then life was sweet. Of course, I was trying to convince myself that this would be the week I would break the cycle and go alcohol-free, although as always, I made sure the opportunity was still there just in case. Anyway, surely a few beers after hours of walking was healthy compared to slumping in a chair with a bottle of wine having sat at a desk all day. *Yes, that was it, why did I not think of that before, I would gradually wind down my alcohol consumption as the week progressed and by the time we reached Stranraer at the end of the walk I would be a*

30

*born-again Christian who only indulged in the occasional sip of sherry at Christmas.* Maybe I could even go on breakfast television and become one of those smug bastards who had found God and was now teetotal.

We stumbled out of the station and onto the path that followed the road into the village. The fact that our farmhouse Bed and Breakfast lay a mile away on the other side of the scattered houses had seemed exciting before we left Southern Suburbia. I had imagined a leisurely stroll in the sun as we wandered our carefree way passed the houses to base camp one. The street lined with smiling locals all waving in admiration at the intrepid explorers; flags hanging from every house to celebrate our arrival. The reality was the incessant cold rain and not a soul in sight. Some life flickered as we passed cars parked outside the local pub, but the small array of shops had long since closed as the evening gloom descended. The main street still had the look of a village in winter hibernation, reluctant to show its soul to outsiders until the sun would break through the blackened sky later in the year. We were just about to turn around and head back to the pub when I spied the lights from a small convenience store shining out into the street at the edge of the village. Harvey charged in, his words tumbling out as though he had just survived a near-death experience rather than ten minutes of typical Scottish weather. "Can you tell us how far it is to Dun

Craig Farm Bed and Breakfast? Please say it's next door." The young boy, well maybe he was a man, but it was all relative to my thinking replied in a thick Dumfrieshire accent that we had a half a mile to go on the main road. Harvey looked at him despairingly, "Half a fucking mile! Can you get a bus to it?"

I thanked the youngster, but he had already dismissed us and was back to concentrating on his smartphone. Watching young people on phones made me feel inadequate; they always smiled to themselves as if caught in a deep and caring conversation with an endless list of friends, their fingers a blur of pressing and prodding as they multi-tasked with the world. How could this generation ever be lonely when they spent so much time talking without speaking? But maybe that was it, take the phone away and they reverted to quiet sullen teenagers trying to find their place in the world the same as every other human being.

It brought home to me what I had really let myself in for when even the process of leaving the dry convenience store became a burden. Worryingly the street lights petered out at the edge of the village long before our half a mile was completed. In the gloom, the last building I could make out was one of those old garages you will only see in remote villages. The one lonely petrol pump had obviously not seen use in years, but the small building still had a sign, *REPAIRS and MOT READINESS* swinging forlornly in the wind. I could vaguely make out a car scrap yard in the field behind it, rusting wrecks that had once been loved by someone but were now sinking back into the mud to allow nature to slowly eat away man's labor and reclaim its own. Modern Britain has seen the demise of car scrap merchants selling spares, the new models have become far too reliable and disposable for anyone to ever think of going to pull off bits from a rusty wreck to fit back onto your own rusty wreck. I left the sight of the lonely metal hulks and hurried after my cursing companion who despite being only a few yards ahead was beginning to disappear in the damp gloom.

In my panic to catch up, I almost ran into the stationary Harvey who was standing peering over an unkept garden hedge. "This must be Dunvaig Ralph, Christ would it be so hard for them to put a bloody light outside? It's supposed to be a fucking bed and breakfast. Castle Dracula would be more welcoming than this place." It was hard not to laugh at Harvey's high-pitched expletive-fueled rant, we had only walked a mile from the station and already he sounded as though he had been to hell and back. Looking over the hedge I could just make out the dark shape of what had once been an imposing and affluent two-story farmhouse. We scrambled through the untidy garden and rattled on the heavy wooden door, but the sound reverberated back to us as though the thick wood was mocking our attempt to be heard. I wiped one of the damp windows with my hand and tried to look inside but its blackness just reflected my face back to me refusing to reveal any of its internal secrets. Just as Harvey was about to break out into another tirade of swearing I noticed a small sign nailed to the door, *Bed and Breakfast guests please use the side entrance.*

"Holy Christ, you would need night vision to find your way to this fucking place" was Harvey's measured response as we edged around the farmhouse searching for signs of life. Eventually, we found a gate leading to an annexe at the back with a beacon of light shining out from one of those old-fashioned lamps attached to the wall. "Ralph old chap no pissing around, let's get booked in, dump our bags and get to the boozer." Of course, I did not need to answer, Harvey was just stating the obvious as we shuffled up to the back door and rattled impatiently on the glass.

Marian was a true eccentric of that there could be no dispute. Even though the kitchen was warm, her ancient frame was covered in layer after layer of clothing including knitted fingerless gloves and a wooly hat, all topped off with a pair of oversized green wellingtons that spouted large white socks cascading over the sides in countless folds. Her face was a mass of lines and furrows making her look as though she had stepped out of a time machine from another century. She could talk like no other human being I had ever encountered.

We sat at the kitchen table in the annexe of the farmhouse listening to her non-stop chatter while enjoying the heat from a real coal fire. Even Harvey sat dumbstruck for once as she made us tea and told us about her life, the farm and the village. I made the mistake of asking her who the men were in the black and white photographs scattered around the room and off she went on another endless tirade. Harvey looked at me as though to say, *shut the fuck up, this is wasting good drinking time,* but I was enjoying winding him up and to be fair Marian did have a charm that washed over us after having battled through the dark cold outside. I nodded to Harvey and he smiled back, the first glimmer of a bond forming between us, the first flicker of understanding that we were in this together.

Our host finally took a breath between talking and we grabbed the opportunity to ask her to take us up to our rooms. I half expected Marian to lead us through the endless corridors holding a candle but contrary to Harvey's comment from this morning, they had discovered electricity in Dalgowan. The whole house felt like a fifties time warp, once the décor would have been a thriving family home, now it felt musty and damp. The walls of the hall and the bedrooms were covered with flowered wallpaper that reminded me of visiting my grandparents' house when I was a child in the early sixties. My room had an old two-bar electric fire but no radiators and a large double bed that was covered in decorative throws and various small flowered cushions. Why did women always feel the need to fill a bed up with innumerable embellishments that had absolutely nothing to do with the actual process of sleeping? Meg did the same and each night I would have to go through the ritual of piling up the cushion ornaments at the side of the bed, so I could get under the duvet. These ones felt cold and smelled of damp as though they had been on the bed waiting to be moved for months, maybe even years. I changed out of my wet clothes and tried to arrange them to dry in front of the orange glow. For the first time since I had dozed off hours ago on the train, I felt some cheer and excitement coming back into my chilled body. Maybe it was because we had finally arrived at the starting point for our long walk, but I had the feeling it was more to do with the fact that we would soon be heading off to the pub and I could let the alcohol haze wash over me.

The familiar sound of a train rattling into the village came through the window and ambling over to the glass I cupped my hands around my eyes and strained to peer out into the black night. So much for the railway expert Harvey who had told me we would be on the last train into Dalgowan. In the distance I could clearly make out the light shining from the two carriages as they slowed to stop at the station. The train looked completely empty, but I thought I could just make out what looked like a single shape standing or was it crouching at the last window? I assumed it must be the guard, what a lonely and boring job that must be at this time of night.

I decided to go out into the gloomy landing hall to look for my companion and hopefully enjoy the consolation of finding that his room was as cold and miserable as mine. Laying half under the bedroom door into my room was a small piece of paper, like one of those notes you used to post as a kid to your mum to say, *sorry for being a brat; can I go out and play with my friends now*? I picked it up and unfolded it while feeling it was odd that it had gone unnoticed when I first came into the room. The yellow molding paper had an erratic scribble across it obviously drawn by a child as well as damp marks as though to confirm it had been written many years ago. The writing was almost inelegible but still made that sort of abstract sense that only a child can make, and a parent can understand. It seemed to read, *sorry mum my money fell into the water* and then a name that could have been Miko or Milo. Carefully folding the little note, I pulled open one of the stiff wooden drawers of the ancient dressing table and placed it inside. For some reason, it did not feel right to mention it to Marian, no doubt it was from when her children had been very young and anyway it would only give her a lead in to tell me another endless story. The voice in my head was already saying, *who gives a fuck, let's find Harvey and get some serious drinking done. We are going to need it trying to sleep in this damp ridden hole.*

I found Harvey's room at the end of the landing and knocked gently on the door before walking in. The lucky bastard had a three-bar electric fire and had already converted the place into home with wet clothes and luggage scattered everywhere. I scanned the room with amusement laced with a hint of admiration, how could anyone make one of Marian's untidy rooms look even more untidy? Harvey sat on the bed cursing as he tried to put his boots back on ready for the mad dash to the nearest pub. "Let's get the fuck out of here and don't ask Brenda or whatever her name is a single question, I swear to God Ralph you were trying to wind me up by keeping her going. Lovely old lady but by Christ does she ever stop fucking talking." It was obvious that Marian's family had long gone, and she ran this place alone. We had been the first guests of the year and it would be hard to imagine the place being busy even in the summer unless it was a few scattered walkers. Even if the odd tourist did stop by it would be unlikely they would be raving on Trip Advisor about the accommodation. *Fantastic musty rooms with state of the art two-bar electric fire and countless damp cushions.* It suited walkers because it was cheap I suppose.

The journey back into the village seemed so much easier without the rucksacks and heavy clothes, even the rain had taken a rest to let the cold wind attack all by itself. For such a small village we noticed that it had both a Chinese takeaway and a fish and chip shop. "Jamie Oliver will be shitting himself when he hears about the competition," I shouted through the wind at the lurching figure of my companion who had his woolen hat pulled down so far it virtually covered his whole head.

"You can keep fucking Jamie Oliver, I am waiting until Nigella Lawson arrives," came the muffled reply from the walking hat. The choice of chef could wait though as another swinging sign read *Belhaven Best* and our real destination of the day had arrived, The Crail Inn. I was not sure what we would see as we opened the door to the bar but the sight that greeted me was both unexpected and oddly familiar. In the south they paid designers to make pubs look old-fashioned; this one did it naturally by simply existing in its own time warp. Padded oak benches clung to the side of each wall to surround five old wooden tables with equally ancient chairs tucked beneath them. The padding had once carried a deep maroon pattern, but years of use had worn most of it away and the shade was now more of an insipid red with white patches where the thread had worn through. The whole bar had a yellowy brown hue from years of smoke stains pervading every corner. The walls were adorned with grainy photographs of what looked like nineteen sixties or at best seventies darts teams, all moustaches and long hair. Men of the time throwing darts and drinking pints while eyeing up the birds. I imagined our landlady Marian walking from the farm to here an eternity ago when she was a spritely young thing arm in arm with one of the young men in the black and white pictures. Now the bar, the farm and Marian had all stopped in time and decided to let the years roll by without them on board. Maybe they understood it was too late to catch up and that trying to do so might wake up Father Time who would quietly tap them on the shoulder and apologetically say, "Oh dear Marian, I completely forgot you are still alive. A complete oversight on my part, time to pop your clogs I'm afraid, oh and while you are at it can you ask that ancient pub and the farm to join you."

Just four people populated The Crail Inn including the barman. He leaned on the bar listening to the conversation of the only three customers with a resigned smile that could only come from having seen the same scenario played out year after year. It was the other three people that surprised me, two young women, in fact, girls because one of them barely looked sixteen while the other looked older, taller and more confident but was probably also only sixteen. Both were obviously very drunk, in fact, the younger looking one was swaying on the bar stool as though she might fall off at any minute and go crashing to the floor. The trio of customers was oddly completed by a man who looked to be in his sixties but was probably a lot younger. He too was well gone but the difference being that years of drinking had given him the ability to keep standing while continuing to talk in that alcoholic scramble that sort of makes sense even though the words don't quite fit into linear sentences.

It did not take long for Harvey to be sitting at the bar talking to the young women. The taller one was called Steph and her companion was Anna. They both wore those ridiculously short dresses that young women wear as though they need to prove to the world that they are feminine and grown up. Steph carried it off with an air of confidence that would no doubt have the young men in the village queuing up to ask her out but on Anna, it looked obscene, as though someone had dressed a child in a woman's clothes. Harvey was already enjoying an audience but once he started telling the girls about the awful bed and breakfast we had booked into I decided to jump in just in case he offended their granny or some other relative. I changed the subject and asked the girls what their story was as they seemed overdressed for an evening in The Crail. It transpired that they had planned a celebration night in the nearest big town Dumfries but had not made it out of the village. Steph chatted away while Anna continued to sway about on the bar stool while still demanding her friend buy another round of drinks. They both claimed to be eighteen although whether that was just to keep the charade going I was not sure. It was obvious the barman knew them anyway but to tell a stranger from out of town that they were underage would have forced his hand to comply with the law and he would have probably been compelled to ask them to leave I suppose. It seemed they were finishing up at school and both would be going to university after the summer. Steph told me with drunken pride that they would be one of the few if not the only local girls in their year that would go to Glasgow to study rather than settle down in Dalgowan like all the others, have kids, become fat and drink themselves to an early grave. Her drunken enthusiasm and vivacious nature made the story seem exciting and conjured up pictures of her poring over dusty books in the university library while questioning bearded lecturers about the meaning of the universe. Anna, on the other hand, seemed surly and unfriendly but I could tell she was shy and in awe of her friend who carried an air of confidence and poise. The old drunk was called Gal and every now and then he would jump in with a comment, usually it would be some lewd suggestion or insinuation to the girls, but Steph laughed it off and fired back friendly comments to him as though it was an acceptable part of this night's or maybe every night's performance.

"Watch yourself there Ralph old boy, I think the volcano might be about to erupt." I had almost forgotten Harvey was sitting beside me having become so engrossed in talking to the girls. The glow of alcohol was beginning to hit us both. *Let's not overdo it tonight, it's going to be a long walk tomorrow, we need to be fighting fit and up early in the morning* had been the chat as we left the farmhouse. We were already onto pint number six and the night was but young.

"What the fuck are you talking about?" I fired back.

"Anna, look at the fucking colour of her face, she is whiter than Mother Teresa's Sari." With perfect timing, the ashen-faced Anna stood up and started to stagger to the ladies with Steph following closely behind her to help. The girls disappeared through a doorway that presumably led to the toilets while Gal and the barman continued with the evening as though this was a perfectly normal occurrence for The Crail. After ten minutes the young women did not reappear and Gal who had finally noticed they had gone made some mixed-up comment about going to the ladies to see if they needed help. The barman laughed while wiping the bar with a dirty cloth,

"You stay away fae those ladies' toilets Gal or I will be having tae bar ye again."

Harvey continued to hold court with Gal, the two of them talking at each other rather than having a conversation while the barman leaned on his chin and tried to make sense of it all. I decided to leave the madness and go to the toilet mainly to use it but also because my nose was bothering me about what had happened to the night's entertainment, Steph and Anna.

I made my way through a dim corridor at the rear of the building and noticed another exit out into the side street. There was no sign of the girls, so I disappointedly assumed that they had made their escape through the back. Inside the gents were cold and the damp smell of urine seemed to seep out of the wet brick walls. The faint hint of an air freshener could just be discerned as though occasionally, a cleaning agent had been spread around to give the impression the place was occasionally visited by the bar staff, a quick spray once a week, job done. Standing over one of the urinals that ran in a line beneath the tiny barred windows my senses picked up a light scratching sound coming from outside almost as if it was directly in front of me behind the brick wall of the toilet. In my drunken state, I was sure that whatever was making the noise was crawling up the wall towards the little window above the urinal. Almost at the same time, I could hear what I thought was the bar door open and voices, *Good that must be the girls back*, I thought to myself while also deciding not to hang around to see whatever was outside, probably a large rat. The tiny sink only produced freezing cold water and the one paper towel dispenser had dispensed long ago. I did that thing that men do, run the tips of your fingers under the water for two seconds so you feel you at least have some hygiene standards. Maybe woman do that as well but don't admit to it. I always imagine women's toilets must be more luxurious, scented candles and dim lighting with fluffy towels. Not in the Crail Inn though, even I knew that.

To my surprise and disappointment, the bar population remained the same as when I had left. Harvey and Gal were chatting away to each other like two long lost friends, both enveloped in that alcoholic fog that bonds drunks together as though they are blood brothers. Although Gal was animated, and words came out of his mouth, his face looked blank, almost expressionless, the face of a man who was really taking nothing in, the face of a dead man whose brain had been eaten away by years of alcohol abuse. "Who came in, I heard the door open?" I asked.

"No one old boy, only fucking zombies are going to be out on a night like this," replied Harvey. For the first time on our trip I felt a sense of strange unease, I had definitely heard voices, the door, and what the hell had been outside, something was playing on the edge of my memory, but I could not fit it in place.

*Shit*...the door burst open and a rush of cold air blew in to add to the shock. I had almost jumped off my seat as I turned around, but it was only Steph. "Sorry Gal, its Anna, she puked up all over the lady's toilets, I had to clean the silly bitch up, fucking told her to slow down but she never listens. I need to go back to make sure she is alright but just wanted to say goodnight. What a fucking great university sendoff

45

celebration eh?" She took it in turns to give Gal, Harvey and me a farewell cuddle. By now drink was starting to take a hold of my reasoning and I had entered that stage where my brain decides I need to show everyone how clever I am and give them fatherly advice even if they don't want it.

"Follow your dream Steph, get out of this village and go to university, promise me you will?" Steph laughed, her face glowing with youth and still untarnished by time.

"Damn right Ralph, no way am I staying in this pit for the rest of my life," she replied. "Well I am going to come back this time next year and I had better not find you still in this pub or anywhere near this village," I said back.

For few seconds, she held my gaze, a sad glint in her expressive blue eyes but that fleeting moment said everything. Now we both knew that Steph and Anna would never leave for university and would remain in the village for the rest of their lives.

After the girls left, the evening fell way into the blur of tangled memories that come after you move into the dangerous territory of not being able to count the number of drinks you have consumed. I vaguely remembered Gal trying to convince us in his brain dead alcoholic language that there was a more exciting bar further back in the village and then the comedy of trying to follow him zig-zagging up the road. Of course, by then Harvey and I would have probably been doing the sideways shuffle as well as we staggered along in search of Dalgowan's best pub according to Gal. The Outhouse was a slightly more affluent version of The Crail and even had a few people inside eating dinner. That was about as far as we got though as the hefty looking blonde bar woman marched Gal back out of the pub while reminding him had he forgotten he was barred again last week for loitering in the women's toilets. She was not over friendly with us either, so we retreated to The Crail but as a bonus, we managed to lose Gal on the way and become the only two customers for the rest of the evening in what had probably always been Dalgowan's best pub anyway.

We finally staggered out of The Crail after midnight having pushed the barman as far as we could go to keep serving us drinks. He had tried to drop hints from eleven onwards by tidying glasses away and counting money in the till, but we simply carried on drinking and ignored the distraction in our hour of need. Of course, by then the chance of getting anything to eat was looking dubious but to our delight, the Chip shop was still in the act of closing for the night. Harvey looked at the plastic letters on the board above the empty looking glass panels that ominously only displayed a frazzled looking battered fish and a lonely looking smoked sausage. "No point in looking at the board son," said the woman behind the counter,

"Its ok mum we just want whatever you have left," replied Harvey.

"You will be getting fuck all if you give me any more of your cheek, all we have is what you see in the cabinet in front of you, it's after midnight and we are wanting to go home."

The words were delivered in that sharp sort of tone that implies it's an order rather than a statement. She was dressed in a greasy looking blue overall that had obviously seen better days but in comparison to the white one her partner wore, it was positively sparkling. He stood in front of the deep fat fryer turning the last remnants of the chips while spots of grease flew out to add to the speckled design on his once white coat. Taking what they had we beat a hasty retreat out into the cold to devour our culinary feast.

"That was a smart fucking thing to say, Harvey, she almost closed the shop on us your daft idiot." My companion grinned,

"I think she fancied me Ralphy boy, all the old grannies do.

The only shelter available to eat our food was one of those small half covered Perspex bus stops. It had an open face out onto the road and freezing metal seats just to add to the pleasure. In our alcohol-addled state, we probably talked away in that Gal style language that only two drunks could understand. We did agree on one point though, if this was the village at the end of the world then the two Southern softies who had arrived that evening had hardly introduced a sense of sophistication onto the streets of Dalgowan. That was the reality though, alcoholics could live in a mansion or a tent, London or Dalgowan, eventually, they would always bring things down to their level. We did finish the evening with a slight touch of class though when Harvey carefully positioned the barely touched dried up chips in the bin beside the bus stop. I had half expected him to hurl them in disgust out into the road while uttering endless expletives.

Even as we staggered through the black night back towards the farm I knew tomorrow was going to be a tough day. The plan to have a few beers and be in bed by ten o'clock had been well and truly dumped. "Do you think your girlfriend Betty or whatever the fuck her name is will open the bar up at the farm for us when we get back Ralphy boy?", the words drifted in the wind towards me from the shadows mocking my concern about the following day. We bumped, crashed and giggled our way through the farmhouse like two schoolboys to finally find our rooms after a few wrong turns. There was one thing that I remembered most from our long first day though as I collapsed fully clothed onto the top of the bed in a drunken haze. It was not the journey or Harvey or Steph or Gal or even the never-ending cold. It was the two piercing green eyes that watched us from inside one of the rusting cars in the scrap yard as we lurched back to the farm in the dark. Their ghostly inhuman glow followed us from a distance as we stumbled past, but I was too drunk and cold to react or to care. It was only when the drink fueled dreams took over that they came back to haunt me during the long night.

## Car Graveyard

Metallic, shiny, once loved

King of the B road, once someone's pride, once someone's joy

Rusted, grass-grown, lonely except for its silent decaying friends.

No piston roar, no ignition spark, just memories of happy miles tread


Metal, rubber, glass, once polished, once caressed

King of the A road, once someone's friend, once someone's desire

Broken, going, merging back into the earth

No piston roar, no ignition spark

Just a mirror of time, just a bearer of life.

## 3- I Drink

The room felt even colder in the pale morning light as I watched my breath exit the only part of my body that was not deeply ensconced under the bed covers. For the moment I felt ok but that was probably due to still being drunk from the night before and no doubt the hangover would soon kick in once I was up and about. A phone was ringing from somewhere in the farmhouse, it was that once familiar old-fashioned bell sound you used to get from those ancient black Bakelite phones that disappeared in the sixties. I wondered if today's generation would look at it in disbelief, *what sort of apps will it support; what spec is the camera; it's a bit bloody big to fit inside your handbag* and so on. A muffled voice was holding a conversation somewhere downstairs on the old phone, the person sounded anxious as though they were impatient to end the call although it was impossible to make out what was being said. The phone went down with what sounded like an angry bang and I went back to contemplating how I was going to get out of the bed without hypothermia kicking in.

I could hear what I assumed was Harvey thumping around in one of the rooms so gritting my teeth I made a dive towards the electric fire to flick the switch and get some warmth. The pathetic glow radiated a surprisingly good heat and allowed me to stay alive while doing a contortionist act to get dressed as painlessly as possible. The shared bathroom in the hall would have to wait as the thought of undressing again to wash in this cold was beyond comprehension. The door to Harvey's room was slightly open so I barged in unannounced while hoping not to have to witness anything embarrassing. He was standing staring through the window that looked out onto the back of the house with a view of the winding road and parallel railway hugging each other in the distance. "What's so interesting?" I half shouted causing him to jump in surprise and jerk around.

"For fuck sake, you could have knocked, you scared the shit out of me you stupid bastard." It was hard not to laugh, I have yet to meet anyone who does not get enjoyment from watching someone jump with surprise although I will admit I fail to see the funny side if it's me as the victim. Harvey recovered his composure and replied in a surprisingly defensive tone as if he had been caught in the act of watching for something that he did not want me to see.

"Nothing, I was just admiring the morning view. Anyway, look down there in the back garden, one of your old girlfriends has followed you from Chelmsford."

I wandered over to stand beside him to look out of the window knowing full well I was about to be on the end of some crude joke. Outside in what must have once been a large vegetable patch was a bedraggled scarecrow dressed in the ragged remains of some castaway clothes. It had fallen half way forward to now lie at a grotesque angle with its face hidden under an old woolen bonnet, almost as though it was trying to kiss the weeds that had grown up around it.

"I went out with worse before Meg felt sorry for me", I joked as we left the bedroom and crept down the stairs looking for the dining room or wherever our host was due to deliver our breakfast. Why is it that every time you stay in a new hotel or Bed and Breakfast it is always impossible to find the dining room and you are forced to wander about opening doors and occasionally bumping into other guests? *Any idea which way it is to the dining room?* To be followed by the reply, *no we are looking for it as well, have been for days now.*

Marian's bright incessant chatter lit up the faded dining room as she served us a massive fried breakfast, just what we needed to help clog up our arteries after a hard night of drinking. She was dressed in that random fashion that elderly people develop to survive the cold. It no longer matters if colours match or if the clothes even fit, just pile one on top of the other to keep the heat in and the cold out. Her outfit looked as though she had walked into a charity shop and just picked up the first ten items from the rail and put them all on. The ornaments that covered every available space in the dining room looked like one of those shelves you find in Cancer Research were nothing matches anything else. I felt tempted to ask her how much the ceramic cat was, or would she do a deal on the Charles and Di plate but decided it might be in bad taste.

I felt awful, this was exactly what I had promised myself would not happen but as usual, once the first drink had gone down I was hooked. The plan had been to walk more than twenty miles to hopefully reach the next tiny village of Blackcraig and avoid having to camp on our first day. Already I was formulating plan B that would see us stay overnight at the lonely John's Cross bothy and cut the day's journey to only 12 miles. Of course, I did not mention this to Harvey as I hoped he would also be suffering from last night's overindulgence and would welcome the compromise. The problem was he seemed incredibly bright and had even engaged Marian in conversation as though last night's drinking session had been just a taster for him before he set out on a leisurely twenty-five-mile stroll. Listening to their conversation it dawned on me how little I knew about Harvey other than he liked a drink and had somehow ended up being my walking companion. I had never really asked him anything about his background or history and listening to them chat made me feel guilty about how little effort I had made to get to know what made him tick. I suppose in my defense I could add that Harvey knew very little about me as well, the deepest question he had ever asked was, "Ralph old chap, is it your round or mine?" For once Marian stopped talking as Harvey told her he had recently split with his girlfriend Sammy and was finding life difficult without her. Problems back home had started to mount up and he had been desperate to get away from the city and find some solitude in the hills. "I had been hoping to get away on my own, but Ralph's wife begged me to come on this trip with him in case he got lost or maybe met a colony of angry penguins in the forest." Marion looked at me sympathetically while Harvey winked in my direction with a friendly grin on his face. I had hoped the conversation would continue and I could find out what problems Harvey was having but Marian had already beaten her lifetime record of not speaking for five minutes and we were soon back to her life on the old farm and the absent family.

As she talked I looked at the monochrome photographs scattered around the kitchen. The handsome young man dressed in a sharp nineteen fifties suit standing proudly with his arm around a young Marian while two small boys sat at their feet in shorts and matching knitted jumpers. No doubt the man would be long dead now and the boys would probably be older than me. She spoke of the children as though they were still around, away out doing the chores on the farm or getting ready for school. It was hard to match the vivacious young girl in the picture with the old woman hunched in front of us talking at a hundred miles an hour while she placed more toast onto the already massive pile in the middle of the table. "So, do you get to see the boys and their families very much?" Harvey asked her.

"Oh yes, they are very good to me, do you know I am now a great-grandmother?" but somehow the answer seemed rushed as though she was trying to defend her offspring rather than compliment them and we wondered how long it really was since any of her family had been to visit.

I poured some tea from the pot that was enclosed in a knitted cover to keep it warm. The kitchen table was a mass of plates and cutlery all set out in some ancient ritual order. Every surface in the dining room was covered in pictures and ornaments, jumble and clutter everywhere, each one of them a part of Marian's past. Gone was the hustle and bustle of children and voices to be replaced by musty dust covered silence. That was why Marian talked so much, she had to get her words out during the time she had a few guests, once we had gone she would be back to her memories and the ghosts who shared the farmhouse with her. Harvey was looking at me; "Time to go, old boy, twenty plus miles and only eight hours of light to get them done." His smile seemed to taunt me but also had a hint of sympathy; *why in God's name was he so bright when the bastard had drunk as much as I had?* Mind you how could I really know? Yet again most of the night after the girls had left had become the usual blank for me. Despite my best intentions I had once again crossed that line in the sand meaning I drank because I had to rather than I wanted to.

Struggling with our cumbersome rucksacks we attempted to squeeze out of the hallway door without sending Marian's endless array of coat stands, umbrellas and neatly lined up old boots tumbling across the floor. Our host came to see us off as though we were the long-lost family that she had only just rediscovered. I wondered if she performed this ritual with every guest, probably in the same way she had done with her boys when they left the nest with their cases packed all those years ago. She gave Harvey a farewell hug as he turned to scramble out of the door and then did the same with me. Was it my imagination that she held onto me longer as though waiting until my companion was out of earshot before quietly whispering, "You don't need to go on this journey son, you already have what you are looking for, leave him to find his own destiny, it will only lead to heartache." Her words unnerved me; she had seemed eccentric rather than crazy, but now I had my doubts. Holding onto her I could feel how thin she was beneath the layers of clothes she covered herself in; there was nothing underneath except frail bones held together by worn skin.

I whispered back "thank you" and turned to leave. Unlike Steph, I knew if I returned to the village next year I would find Marian gone, the village finally releasing her spirit to soar away over the hills and forests. Then the farm would stand nervously waiting to greet its next line of heirs as a skip lay in the driveway full of broken memories. The black and white picture frames smashed but the boys in their knitted jumpers still smiling out from the disintegrating photographs amid the ruin.

We walked out into a damp grey day but for once the rain remained held in the clouds floating menacingly above us. The small cluster of buildings seemed to be hemmed in on all sides by the brooding hills and the vague dark shadows of distant forests. It was as if they kept the village hostage, watching their every move as if daring the inhabitants to try and escape from the little valley. The Southern Upland Way cut through the North end of the village just before the train station and allowed us to check in at the shop for provisions. The young man from the night before had been replaced by a young woman; of course, she took our money while tapping away on her phone. Maybe she was texting Gal to report that the two Chelmsford pussies who had ditched him last night had arrived back in town. I decided for once in my life to be sensible and purchased water and aspirins while Harvey rummaged around the shelves looking for heaven knows what. We passed the scrap yard and the garage which remained closed. The remnants of a dead crow lay flapping in the wind on the old forecourt as if something had been feasting on it and had suddenly been disturbed. No doubt the predator would return later to finish the carcass off. For some reason I tried not to look as I felt uneasy, but my mind was too focused on trying to walk without being sick to really let it bother me. As we marched passed the Crail Inn and the sign for the train station the same feeling crept over me, something did not feel right but I had no idea what it was. Maybe the something was me being here in the middle of nowhere with a stinking hangover and a walk of more than twenty miles to complete. I probably just needed a drink!

I decided to do my duty and called Meg before we set out. She chattered for ten minutes about her friend Caroline who was in the hospital with terminal cancer. I listened and tried to insert sympathetic words at the correct point to show I was a caring human being. We knew Meg was really talking to herself though. It was not that I did not care; it was just that I lacked the ability to empathize, or the personal skills required to feel real emotion. Women just seemed to have more feelings than men, we tried but, surface talk was all most males seemed to be able to muster. It was as if talking about a horrible disease would make it more likely we would catch it. For some reason, if Meg was watching a program about surgery or obesity I would always have to leave the room or shield my eyes in case the disease jumped out of the screen and landed on me. I had never been in a pub with other men and discussed how we really felt. We did not even mention our children unless it was to moan about the cost of a wedding or our daughter's new boyfriend. I had however spent endless hours chatting about football or who would like to join me on a crazy hiking adventure while either being verbally assaulted or verbally assaulting. Maybe that was the difference between men and woman; males could openly insult each other and laugh, if that happened in female company blood would flow. Could it be that men were allowed to remain children all their lives meaning the women had no choice but to become the adults? Maybe the truth was that men just acted like children, so their partner would do most of the work. Except put the bins out or do the barbeque of course, that is male territory.

We turned off the main road and climbed over a rickety overgrown wooden style to finally join the Southern Upland path. This was our first warning that there was no actual path, just the very occasional half decaying post sticking out of a bog or at the side of a hill telling us we were heading in the right direction. When the path first opened in a blaze of publicity many years ago it had been well signposted and forest rangers looked after sections in anticipation of the thousands of walkers who would descend on the track each week. This of course never happened and gradually it had reverted to nature unloved and rarely visited but that added to the romantic charm and the feeling of isolation. I decided to introduce my caring female side and enquire what Harvey had been alluding to when he told Marian that he had problems back home and needed to get away. Maybe it was too early in our relationship to delve into his private life, but I was surprised at the almost cold dismissive response I received. "Nothing, it's nothing don't ask." So much for trying to show depth and understanding, I would have been better asking him if he fancied one of the sheep grazing on the moor nearby. He knew he had been short in his reply and immediately tried to make things light again.

"Guess what I have in my rucksack, Ralph?"

"An Indian Elephant," I replied sharply, still feeling annoyed at his put down.

"No, a fucking full bottle of Johnnie Walker whisky, we could stop half way today and stay in the bothy at John's Cross and tan it. Break the journey up as I know you are feeling a bit fragile. Make up the miles later in the week. What do you reckon Ralph old boy?" The words were hardly out of his mouth before I had forgiven him. The offer by Harvey to break the journey without me having to ask him was good enough but to throw in a bottle of scotch as a bonus proved he was a class act. That's what I meant about men being shallow I suppose.

Our destination for the day included a torturous hike towards the summit of Benrack at nearly 2000 feet although we would not reach the top until after our overnight camp. Any concerns I had about Harvey being too fast for me quickly disappeared. I had headed upwards towards what looked like either mist or low-lying cloud keeping as comfortable a pace as I could and on turning around I noticed Harvey was already struggling and had fallen well behind. Sitting on a mound of damp grass gave me the opportunity to look back down the track at the slow-moving hulk steadily dragging its way up the steeply ascending moorland. It made me wonder why he had ever wanted to come on this walk in the first place; an overweight middle-aged man who loved to drink. He did not even seem to enjoy the scenery or even being out in the wilds and yet he was still here. It did not make sense but then I had no idea why I was doing this either, sitting halfway up a hill in the middle of nowhere freezing to death. Who the hell was I to question his motives, fucked up Ralph with no sense of future or direction in life? Behind the still distant figure of Harvey, I could see the panorama of the little village spread out before me, the railway snaking like a contortionist as it headed through the hills that enclosed Dalgowan on both sides. My eyes strained to see the tiniest of black dots moving along the road towards where we had turned off and crossed over the style. Just as the mist closed in and blocked my view I could tell the figures had taken the style and started on the path to follow in our tracks. It could only be other walker's, but it seemed strange they would start even later in the morning than us and that we had not met them in the village. It could also mean we would have company tonight in the bothy although given Harvey's current rate of progress it was more likely they would overtake us, and we would end up being their guests.

Harvey finally ambled through the now swirling mist with a grunt followed by "Fuck me this is tough, how far until we get to the bothy and get a drink?" It was beginning to dawn on me that it would need a miracle if he was ever going to cover the one hundred miles we needed to walk to get to the coast and Stranraer.

"I think we may have company," I shouted as he edged towards me. That same look of concern I had seen when he had been looking out of the farm window flashed across his face again. "Yes, I reckon I could see at least another two walkers leaving the village as I waited for you to haul your ass up here."

His good-natured grin quickly returned, "Maybe it's the two girls coming after us because they can't resist my charm." He quipped.

"It's more likely to be Gal." I retorted. "Maybe your undoubted charm worked on him as well, either that or he knows you have a bottle of whisky and he is tracking you down."

"Even if it's the girls they are not touching my fucking whisky," replied Harvey with an ironic grin.

After four hours of continuous climbing through the marshy hillside in thick mist, we finally spied the dark outline of a conifer forest. I had slowed down to allow Harvey to keep up, both of us cursing our way through the wet grass and muddy puddles. Already the wet had penetrated my walking boots but I had quickly accepted that being soaked was less work than trying to dodge around the endless little pools of water. I was already beginning to realize that all day hill walking was miserable unless you fought the miles by concentrating on taking as few steps as possible to cover the required distance. It was a relief to finally enter the forest with its tall trees bunched on either side of the path giving us protection from the damp mist. We tramped on feeling like invaders in this silent eerie world, not a single living thing could be heard not even a bird call. Back in Chelmsford, I had lain in bed at night trying to picture what the walk would be like, for some reason I had imagined endless wildlife, maybe the occasional deer grazing in front of us, birds chattering in the trees. There was nothing, absolutely nothing except the ghostly rustle of wind as it tried to steer a way through the dense mass of conifers. We had only walked for five hours on what had originally been planned as a ten-hour trek when we came around a corner on the forest track and in a clearing stood the outline of a small hut like building. John's Cross bothy welcomed us in all its glory.

But unfortunately, there was no glory. In my guide to the Southern Upland Way, this had been described as the gem of the three shelters we would encounter on our walk. Maybe I had expected it to be larger, but the reality was a brick building about the size of a single garage with a small door at the front and a window on either side. We crept forward feeling like intruders and gently pushed the stiff wooden door open. The spartan interior perfectly matched the uncomplicated exterior. A large wooden table sat in the middle of the single room surrounded by four cheap plastic chairs while a large shelf ran along one side, presumably to be used as sleeping accommodation. The only other embellishments were a few molding pictures hanging on the walls and some damp rotting books probably left by previous visitors. The biggest let down was the lack of a fireplace as well as the realisation that we would have to go outside into the forest to use the toilet. It reminded me of those buildings I used to find abandoned while playing as a child, that smell of damp and dirt that permeates a structure once it has lost its human inhabitants. I could see Harvey also had that look of disappointment on his face and I immediately felt guilty. After all these buildings were supplied free to walkers, what the hell had I really thought I was going to get, a three-star bedroom and an endless walk to find the dining room? What really irked me though was the fact that this was described as the best bothy in my guidebook which meant the other two would be even more stark and miserable. It would have been better if we had initially stayed in the lowest rated one and then we could have dreamed of improving luxury as we trekked further into these desolate hills. I wondered if two less enthusiastic walkers had ever come this way, it was certainly hard to imagine. What in God's name were we doing here, cold and miserable with another 90 miles to go? Harvey pulled out the bottle of whisky as if he was reading my thoughts and collapsed down in one of the plastic seats. "Don't worry Ralph old chap, trust me, this place will look like the fucking Hilton once we down this little beauty," he chuckled as he took a large swig and then passed me the bottle. Things were looking up even if it was only until we finished the whisky.

A guest book sat on the table inside a clear plastic bag with a pen attached to it by a bit of string. I could not resist opening it to read the comments from previous visitors. It seemed we were the first to use the place this year although a trickle of people had written something from the year before. What amazed me on turning the pages, was finding faded words written from as far back as the nineteen eighties. Depressingly the comments all followed the same vein, *lovely well-maintained hut, we had a great night singing campfire songs with our new friends Bob and Jean, this place is magical in the moonlight, what superb amenities and all for free, Jason loves Kylie* and so on. I passed the book over to Harvey along with the whisky bottle, "You might need another drink before you read this crap," I said. I watched in amusement as he turned each page, his face becoming more incredulous with each comment. Finally, he turned the book back to the first blank page and carefully taking the pencil wrote, *this place is worse than a shithole; they should be paying us to stay in this dump.* He then winked in my direction before adding, *Regards, Ralph Casalles, amateur solo hill walker.*

"We need to try and light á fire outside, it's only three o'clock in the afternoon; if we don't we will freeze to death before the night comes," commented Harvey as we passed the whisky bottle backwards and forwards. To be fair the kind guardians of the mountain hut charity had left a metal bin in the clearing outside. Harvey had resumed the role of expedition leader and told me to go scavenge for wood, not too difficult as the stuff was everywhere. I came back feeling good about myself at having the sense to find innumerable dry twigs under the forest canopy at the edge of the clearing. My partner had found a use for the rotting books and soon we had a small blaze going, things started to look up. It's amazing what a fire can do to raise your spirits. Life must have been shit for the cavemen until some bright spark literally did just that and discovered fire. We unpacked our sleeping bags and tried to make the grim interior look like home while bouncing in and out to get a heat from the flames and a swig of the whisky bottle. Our territorial instincts had kicked in as any minute now we expected the other walking party to catch up and demand some of our hard-earned shelf space. It was already agreed that in the unlikely event it was a party of women then they would be welcome, if as expected it was a bunch of wet smelly males then they could have the floor, nothing else and not the whisky.

We need not have worried as dusk soon fell over the wet clearing with no sign of another soul. The two of us continued to scramble about in the dark trying to maintain the fire but the amount of effort involved was starting to overtake the supply of heat being returned back. By eight o'clock in the evening, a freezing mist had started to descend, and we abandoned our fire and retreated inside in a warm drunken haze. But soon the cold started to take hold and we shivered inside our sleeping bags while wearing as much dry clothing as possible. Our small camping stove gave some temporary heat as I tried to boil up tins of sausage and beans. No doubt a naked flame inside the hut was against the rules but if a fire started at least we would go out in a blaze of glory while getting a heat. The whisky did its business though and we talked long into the cold night until the bottle eventually ran dry.

The drink dampened Harvey's defenses and although it was hard going trying to get him to be serious he did open up a bit. He told me he had split with his girlfriend; well she had dumped him after they had moved to Norwich. His track record with women had never been any good, his words not mine. It was not hard to see why, Harvey seemed to treat life like a big game, and responsibility for anything including women and jobs was to be avoided like the plague while maximizing personal enjoyment. And yet listening to him I could sense that he was not happy with his life either. "I should be more like you Ralph, a good marriage, children and take life seriously, the way it should be." The words made me feel hollow and insecure because as he was talking I had been thinking to myself, *I wish I was more like him, able to relax and enjoy the moment instead of always feeling inadequate.* Even as we chatted I felt he was holding back though on the real reason he had joined me on our trek. I knew something had been needling me and maybe that was it. Whatever his problem was I got the impression he had decided to forget about it and there was no way he was going to discuss it with me, well not yet anyway. Two lost alcoholics running from everything and thinking the other one had all the answers to life.

Using the glow from our small camping light, I rummaged through my bag and soon felt the cold glass of the hidden bottle I was searching for fall into the palm of my hand. With a look of triumph permeating across my face I held up the half litre of vodka in front of Harvey who was sitting beside me on the hut shelf wrapped from head to toe in his sleeping bag. I had intended to keep this throughout the 100-mile trek and only produce it if required during a dire emergency, maybe to keep the pain of a broken leg under control or to be taken just before the end as frostbite consumed us. This shit hole of a building was excuse enough though to break out the emergency rations. We both burst into drunken laughter as Harvey followed suit and like a magician pulled out one of those silver hip flasks he had filled with whisky before leaving Chelmsford. "This first Ralphy boy, the vodka will do as a nightcap." It felt good to know that I was working with a drinking professional now; this guy really was right up my street.

I woke up at around two am, the cold was tough, but my head was worse, I was drunk and still would be even in the morning. It was decision time; either suffer all night desperate to go to the toilet or get up and go outside to possibly freeze to death. The thought crossed my mind to just use a corner of the hut, but I knew that even in my current state it would be an insult to all the others who may seek shelter here as we had done. Harvey snored and grunted in his sleep, he would not surface until daylight, I was sure of that. I tried to piece together the end of the evening and vaguely remembered getting a sporadic signal on my phone and calling Meg but could not recall if our conversation had been hopeless due to the mobile connection or my inebriated state. It was probably both. I was sure that sleep had consumed me before we had opened the vodka, but the empty bottle stared back at me beside Harvey. Nothing else for it I thought and pulling the sleeping bag down, I staggered to the door while bouncing against the walls and eventually managed to make it outside like some punch-drunk old boxer. The mist had faded away, but the ground lay frozen and hard as a half-moon doused a deadly light across the clearing. I leaned with one hand on the outside wall while hopefully directing the steaming pee against the building rather than down my legs. As I finished and turned around something made me glance at the path that passed the bothy about ten yards away. My whole body froze in stillness like the statuesque trees; standing silhouetted on the path staring directly at me was a child of no more than seven. But this was no ordinary child, its pallid coloured skin and hollow blackened eyes meant it was a dead child.

I Drink

Bridge, River, Dark, Wet, A place for the broken, a home for
the lonely
Alcohol, Cigarettes, smoke and violence
Clouded memories, you, the children, South Street, home,
hell
Ask me why; go on ask me why I drink.

Black shimmering stagnant water, reflecting the city, image
of my black heart
Lager, Whisky, Woodbine and broken glass
Fading memories, forgotten holidays, old cars, kicked in
doors, crying youth
Tell me why; go on tell me why I drink.

Floating dead dog, sewer rats, all I have, all I ever was
A dram, your round, Police and blood
Distant memories, Aunties, mothers, parties, screaming, late-
night retribution
I don't know why; I don't know why I drink.

So Black River, you have me now, to join your decaying
flock
And those I leave who will not grieve
For you cannot lose what you never had

So, I raise a toast to my only love and embrace my friend the drink.

# 4- Winter's Child

We both woke around 6 am frozen and stiff after a tough night's sleep on the hut's hard wooden shelf. I could feel the intense damp cold on my face although the rest of my body remained covered so long as I did not try to move around in the sleeping bag. Any slight contortion seemed to let the icy fingers of late winter find a passage to infiltrate my bones, so I lay as still as possible while taking in the Spartan surroundings and thinking back to the previous evening. I remembered the vision of the dead child and stumbling back through the dark in drunken terror before hiding deep in my sleeping bag until I drifted away into an uncomfortable sleep. I now knew that drinking was not only affecting me physically, it was also starting to impact my mental state as well. Here I was laying in the cold with a stinking alcohol-induced hangover, while having to contemplate the horror that I was now starting to see things that did not exist. I thought about those books on alcohol addiction that described the poor victims seeing giant spiders crawling up walls while small insects scuttled over their skin; was this coming next? Had it already started? This was it, the last junction in the road before the winding track to oblivion. The last step before I became a mirror image of Gal with my final few living brain cells randomly crashing into each other like a mass of drunk drivers. I had to stop drinking, I simply had to, and of course at that very moment while lying in my sleeping bag racked with guilt and remorse I really meant it, honestly, I really did.

Harvey, as usual, seemed to have no after effects at all from the alcohol. "I don't remember polishing off that bottle of vodka, I must have fallen asleep before you," I said.

"Nah you're kidding, that was definitely you Ralph, you can drink me under the table you are a walking booze bag."

Surely that had to be a joke, an alcoholic elephant would fall down before Harvey stopped drinking, but his comment made me feel uneasy. Maybe it was me who had the real problem and I liked to just think he was worse, maybe my alcoholic elephant was already lying under the table waving a white flag as if to say, *Ralph I surrender, you drink even more than that walking liquor machine Harvey*. If I was starting to see corpses walking around, then forgetting I had drank the room dry was hardly going to come as a revelation. I laughed to myself as I watched Harvey trying to light the portable gas stove to make coffee while still inside his sleeping bag. Any minute now I imagined he was going to crash on top of the tiny stove. Maybe the whole ensemble him included would ignite in a glorious burst of flame taking me and the hut with it. I suppose that would at least have solved my drinking problem.

We agreed the only way to warm up was to set off and get to Blackcraig as soon as possible. By Seven AM the two of us had packed our rucksacks, had coffee and headed out into a cold but dry clear daybreak. I always found the morning cheered me up, even when I had a hangover. In the dim sunlight, the bothy looked like an old friend waving us goodbye. It was an old friend I never wanted to see again of course. I used the last remnants of my phone battery to take a picture of the hut. Maybe back in the comfort of my home I would think back fondly to our night in the bothy, I doubted it though. We continued to the summit of Benrack and then descended through the never-ending conifer trees to finally emerge into open moorland. The sudden shock of being exposed made me realize how all-enveloping the forest had felt, already I was starting to use excuses for the apparition I had seen rather than blame the true culprits, the whisky and vodka bottles. "At this rate, we will make the village by twelve. That is what I call perfect timing old boy, the pubs will just be opening," commented Harvey with a spring in his step.

He seemed to be able to keep up when we descended rather than climbed as for once we managed to walk together at a decent pace. For the first time since leaving London, I started to settle into the walk and even slightly enjoy it. "Let's get to Blackcraig, get a decent hotel to stay in and tomorrow try and do at least 20 miles, maybe get back on track," I enthused.

"Sounds good to me old boy," was the surprisingly positive response from Harvey, without even a hint of sarcasm or humor. I had expected at least a comment about getting pissed in the afternoon, but could it be that even the big man was, at last, starting to think in terms of completing the walk. I almost felt a pang of disappointment at the thought that maybe we really would behave ourselves tonight, somehow, I doubted it though.

We continued to lose height as the track suddenly joined the luxury of a small tarmacked lane. Even the presence of something as mundane as a manmade road was enough to lift our spirits after hobbling through endless hours of wet grass and mud. A few hundred yards to our left stood an ominous looking modern farm. It had no sign of life other than a handful of seagulls floating above what looked like a tarpaulin-covered silage heap. I had always associated seagulls with the sea due to the name, although no doubt they would scavenge anywhere that supplied a free meal. The front of the farmhouse had at least ten hanging baskets attached to the walls full of dried out and rotting plants. It looked like a line of dead soldiers standing guard over the silent farm. It seemed strange that someone would make so much effort to fill the pots up and then not bother to remove them once winter had arrived to kill the flowers off. A feeling of unease started to creep over the two of us, so we hurried past before deciding to take a rest at a little metal bridge that crossed over a gurgling burn.

"Do you know you can drink the water from a stream out here? It's as pure as the driven snow," said Harvey as he peered down into the stream. "Trust me Ralph, this is the same stuff they put into bottles and charge you a fortune for."

"Is that right?" I replied. "Well I tell you what then, you take a big long cool drink of that lovely pure water and I will use up the rest of the bottled water and make myself a coffee on the stove."

My companion wandered over to the edge of the bridge and bent down to look at the flowing burn. Cupping his hands together as though he was a seasoned explorer Harvey scooped up some of the water before abruptly dropping it back into the stream.

"Fuck that, the sheep probably use it as a toilet; make me a coffee with the bottled water as well if you would be so kind Ralph old chap."

While he had been performing this charade, I took one last picture of the great adventurer before my phone made a pathetic spluttering noise and died completely. Of course, how was I to know what was already happening to the image I took that day as the camera's hardware processed the picture. The friendly smiling Harvey I could see through the lens had already started to change in the microsecond it took the impression to move along to the phone's memory card to be replaced by the look of a haunted man, lines of worry etched across his face. The man who just accepted life and tackled it day by day or a least drink by drink now looked out from the photograph with the eyes of a defeated man, staring back into the blackness of no future that awaited us all when our time was over.

The water in the little pan finally started to boil and I poured it carefully into the plastic cups. Just as I lifted one to pass over to Harvey a high-pitched scream like an animal either in pain or fear rendered the air. "Jesus Christ," I shouted, the hot coffee had spilled over my hand. "What in god's name was that?"

"It sounds like the hound of the bloody Baskervilles," replied my frightened looking companion. At least we had both heard it, so I had the comfort of knowing that this time it was not a drink-fueled illusion. The screech was followed by the barking of what was probably a very large and very unfriendly dog coming from the nearby farm. We put it down to being in the countryside and at least it seemed more natural than the deep stillness and nothingness of the forest. Never the less we quickly packed up and moved on just in case the farmer appeared on his horse followed by a pack of bloodhounds chasing the scent of two hopeless Essex alcoholics. The sound of the dog seemed to follow us as we fled and did not subside until we left the road to rejoin the path. Within minutes we had re-entered another manmade forest of fir trees, the all-conquering quiet and stillness rapping its cloak around us once again like an old friend. And yet somehow, I could not help wondering if the woodland was not the real enemy, as if it was shaping the path in front of us, driving the track to the destination it had wanted us to follow from the very start.

The incident with the bloodhounds was quickly consigned to history as the dry and bright weather helped us to amble along in a relaxed manner. I knew Blackcraig could only be three or four hours away and the thought of a warm room and a hot shower added an extra spring to my step. Even the hangover had abated, and my brain was starting to drop hints to my body that maybe I deserved a few drinks later. *Not too many, just a couple, that won't do you any harm.* We said very little as we pounded on, each of us lost in our thoughts until Harvey, never one to push himself too hard, called for another rest stop. We sat down on a fallen tree to take in the eerie silence. My ears strained as the first faint hint appeared of something breaking through the stillness. "Listen, what's that? Can you hear someone coming?" I whispered. The sound was more like a repetitive tapping rather than the beat of footsteps. The rhythmic noise increased as it approached and held me trance-like as I watched with my nerves on edge waiting to see what would appear from around the trees. I had expected Harvey to jump up and make a joke or comment but even he sat like a statue waiting in anticipation for the tapping sound to reveal itself.

Tap, tap, tap, the sound became slightly louder but still seemed distant as though it was afraid to anger the forest by breaking the eerie silence. A man appeared around the corner, he was certainly an apparition but not in the ghostly sense. Despite appearing small and fragile he carried the biggest rucksack on his back that I had ever seen. It was as if the huge pack was being held up by some invisible force rather than the little body that seemed suspended beneath it. It was adorned with every walking implement possible including pots, metal cups, cutlery, a torch and a gas stove. These all hung from a string and covered almost every inch of his walking jacket. Extended in front of his chest was some sort of metal wire contraption that held maps in a plastic sheet, so he could read them by simply looking down. The final piece of the jigsaw was two white walking sticks in each hand that had been making the tapping sound as he paced along. An oversized woolen hat covered his face except for a pair of oval glasses wrapped tightly around his eyes. They reminded of those national health prescription specs that kids wore in the sixties before fashion for children was invented.

Maxime had traveled over from Belgium and started the walk from Stranraer, going in the opposite direction to us. We peppered him with questions as though an escape valve had been released, allowing us to talk to another human being after the intimidating claustrophobia of the forest. For some reason, he was doing the full Southern Upland walk of 200 miles from the West Coast all the way to the East Coast near Berwick, sleeping either in the huts or his small tent. Maxime told us he had done the same walk eight years ago and was now doing it again but other than that he gave very little away and seemed agitated to be off again. He reminded me of a robot, an automaton who simply walked for no other reason than to go through the motion of putting one foot in front of the other for hour after hour. I did not get any sense of enjoyment from him and he gave no hint or reason why he had traveled so far to do the same route again. Within minutes the lonely Belgian was off again but just as he started to disappear around the next bend he turned around and shouted back to us, "You two are the only real walkers I have met since I started out three days ago." With that final comment, he clicked his way onwards and disappeared into the trees. Harvey looked at me and shrugged.

"He thinks you are a walker Ralph, poor guy is obviously deranged."

Maxime's eccentricity cheered us up, a fellow hiker who seemed to be completely enveloped in his own lonely walking world. Maybe that's what the forest and being alone did to you. It took control and emptied your mind, so you became as one with the silent trees; the only thing left to show that you had not blended in completely being the distant click of your walking sticks. Click, click, click, I am still alive, I am still alive, I am still alive, but only just. As he disappeared around the bend I thought of him being alone, sleeping in that bothy, with no one to talk to except the ghosts. I watched Harvey shuffle off the log in front of me to continue our journey and I realised how much I appreciated his company. For the first time I felt a bond, maybe I was beginning to realize why he was here, why he was with me.

A few miles further on we again came out into a clearing and a marked junction on the track. From here on the path became better defined as though it saw more than the occasional use every eight years by strange men from Belgium. A sign pointed right to Ben Lochy Youth Hostel two and a half miles away, but for us that was a reason to continue straight on and avoid it like the plague. I had stayed in a youth hostel once in my life and that was more than enough. The place had been full of cheerful healthy types and every room had an all-pervading smell of baked beans. In the shared kitchen, people sat drinking tea or eating spaghetti on toast, no alcohol in sight of course. Paper signs clung to every wall with clearly displayed rules such as, *no smoking, lights out/ doors locked by ten pm, ABSOLUTELY NO ALCOHOL ALLOWED ON PREMISES* and so on. I am sure Harvey and I might have contemplated the advantages of staying in Ben Lochy hostel for the evening, but you have probably guessed what the problem might be.

The forest started to break, and the trees changed from the endless pine variety to more varied types including Ash and Silver Birch, a sure sign that habitation was looming. This part of the path was obviously used by casual walkers and sure enough, we soon noticed a couple with a dog coming towards us. They looked to be in their early forties, an air of affluence about them. The man nodded a friendly hello and told us we had about a mile to go in what sounded like a Norfolk accent. Harvey stood and watched them as they walked off into the distance. "What's the problem?" I asked. He shrugged his shoulders and started to move on.

"Nothing Ralph, they just seemed familiar for some reason. Maybe it was just the accent."

Strolling into Blackcraig just after midday, we found a straggling little village no bigger than Dalgowan but a welcome sight none the less. The few streets looked deserted except for the occasional car passing through and yet our enquiries for a room at the only two hotels proved fruitless. "Who the fuck stays in a place like this in March, what is wrong with these people?" was Harvey's usual carefully thought out observation.

"Well to be fair we probably met two of them on the track an hour ago for a start", I replied. "Fucking arseholes, have they got nothing better to do than ponce about in in the middle of nowhere, it's fucking mid-winter," snapped back a clearly agitated Harvey.

The irony that we were doing the same as everyone else was lost on my companion as he ranted at the world for not simply having a hotel and a pub fall at our feet the minute we arrived. One of the hotel staff pointed us in the direction of a forest ranger who let out a room to walkers and we soon found the house at the edge of the village. I expected the door to be opened by a man dressed as a Canadian Mountie for some reason but the guy who answered looked nothing like how I had imagined a forest ranger to look. He was dressed like any other middle-aged man, find something you are comfortable in and then wear it forever. Ian had to be the most unenthusiastic forest ranger imaginable; any questions regarding our route tomorrow or the track we had completed were met with one sentence answers. It became clear that he was no Canadian Mountie; Ian just ran a business letting out rooms or picking up walkers and taking their bags to rendezvous points. I got the distinct impression that he had taken the business on, but it had failed to make him his fortune, how could it when we had covered the last two days and met only one other walker. He charged us an astonishing one hundred and eighty pounds for the room although to be fair it was actually a flat with a bedroom, living room/kitchen and bathroom. He could have said Three hundred pounds and we would have still taken it; sleeping in freezing cold huts has that effect on you.

The only comment Ian the Mountie made about the accommodation was to warn us that his elderly mother lived next door and as she had dementia she would occasionally unlock the connecting room door to her flat, so beware in case she wondered in. Never one to miss a trick, Harvey turned to me and whispered, "Looks like this could be your lucky night Ralphy boy." I gave him a sharp look in case our host had heard his comment, but I need not have worried. Mister Forest Ranger was already walking out the door grasping the banknotes we had given him as though he had won the lottery.

We unpacked, cleaned up and left our phones to recharge but it still gave us almost half a day to amuse ourselves. The danger sign was there; all day boozing loomed. I knew I had to at least try to break the cycle even if it was just to delay the inevitable drinking session later. "Not for me Harvey, I need a break. I am going to see if I can find a bus to Dumfries and walk around the town." He looked at me incredulously as I continued my attempt to be sensible for once.

"We need to do 20 miles tomorrow or we will never get back on track, if I start drinking now I won't even see tomorrow, never mind go hill walking." I had hoped he would agree to come with me, but his response left me in no doubt of his intentions.

"Are you kidding, no fucking way am I walking any further than the pub down the road. Come on Ralph, we can do twenty miles tomorrow no problem, join me for a beer old chap, Christ we deserve it. It's a holiday not a slave drive for God's sake."

Despite the temptation, I stuck to my guns and Harvey reluctantly agreed to meet me later for dinner when I got back. I knew he had hollow legs and would still be propping up the bar on my return, as well as having a clear head in the morning. We walked back into the village and I headed over to the bus shelter as Harvey started to disappear through the door of a small pub. He turned around and shouted down the street to me, "I bet this place is full of single women all looking for a night of passion Ralphy boy and you are going to miss out."

"The best you will find in that place will be Gal's twin brother, anyway I am not a real hill walker, as you keep telling me," I called back before he vanished into the bar, no doubt to be molested by all those single women waiting for him inside.

I was impressed with my resolve as I checked over the timetable outside the shelter. Maybe the dead had spooked me more than I was willing to admit but if I was back by six I could still join in the fun. The confusing jumble of tiny numbers written on the poster seemed to indicate a bus would appear in another 40 minutes. There was nothing else to do but sit in the Perspex shelter and watch very little happen in the main village street. Just my luck the weather decided to turn grey and the first drops of rain started to patter onto the roof. I had no real idea why I was heading into the large town of Dumfries other than to try and stem the boredom of a long afternoon and hopefully delay the inevitable decline into another alcohol-induced stupor. A smart black BMW passed and then stopped a hundred yards down the road. It started to reverse back towards the shelter. *Oh, Christ*, I thought. *Here we go. Any minute now a face will appear at the passenger window, some old lady in tweed and pearls.* "Can you tell me how to get to Inverclade estate, we have an appointment with Lord Belvoir," or "Is this the right road to Clachnacluddin House, we are expected for dinner at eight," followed by the inevitable embarrassing few minutes of apologies as I tell them I am from Essex and they laugh politely at their mistake. That's the great thing about being an eternal pessimist though; it means you are never disappointed and sometimes delighted. It turned out to be the couple we had passed a few hours earlier on the track and they had recognized me.

"If you are heading to Dumfries we can drop you off as we are staying in a hotel there," said the friendly male voice of the driver as he leaned across the blonde woman sitting in the front passenger seat.

You could see that Susan had once been a striking looking woman, she still was, but the premature lines emitting from the sides of her eyes told of some deeply hidden sadness. Despite sitting beside her partner Douglas, she seemed aloof, almost as though she existed on another plain. Douglas did most of the talking while Susan would occasionally nod in agreement. I wondered if it was him who made her look so unhappy, but it felt unlikely. He came across as friendly and caring and you could see he held a deep affection for Susan although she seemed cold in response. I tried to stop pretending I could read people and out of politeness asked them what they were doing in Galloway. Douglas grasped at the chance to talk and told me they lived in a small village near Norwich but having been brought up in Dumfries as a boy, they often visited family or holidayed in the area. They had driven up to Blackcraig with Rob their dog to walk for a few hours on the forest track. Rob was a beautiful old golden retriever curled up in a ball in the back compartment of the large estate car. I chatted back and forth with Douglas and occasionally Susan, but inevitably we started to run out of conversation and after a few attempts to fill the embarrassing silence we settled into our roles of driver and passenger. The rain was now falling heavily causing condensation to cover the rear windows as the car plowed along the wet road. We passed through tiny hamlets and countryside, at one point we splashed past the vague shape of a man walking a dog. "God it's not the sort of day to be walking a dog," I said.

Douglas's reply unnerved me, "I don't think anyone would venture out in the rain on this road with a dog, it would be far too dangerous".

I turned around to make sure I had seen the man, but the rain covered rear window made it impossible to see more than a few yards behind.

It took us about an hour to get to Dumfries town centre; it felt good to see traffic and people milling about despite the rain. The main street was littered with familiar American franchises selling coffee and hamburgers. People of my age always seemed to moan about the high street being taken over by the same corporate brands no matter where you went, but what was the alternative? It was either that or boarded up windows and endless charity shops. No doubt I had been hooked by the carefully placed caffeine addiction but what the hell, Regular Americano with cold milk in a plastic cup and I was a happy man. Well at least until the pubs opened.

I tried to strike up a last-minute conversation with Susan who had said very little other than to occasionally agree with Douglas. Just as the car slowed down to drop me off I made one last attempt to lighten the atmosphere, "So have you two got any children or are you happy go lucky and living the life of freedom and money?" The second my pathetic words were out I knew I had said the wrong thing. It was as if time had stopped and even though it was maybe only a few seconds it felt like an eternity, until Douglas jumped in to try and save the day.

"Will this do you here Ralph, it's pretty much the center of the town and best for the shops." I mumbled an embarrassed thank you and goodbye while desperately trying to unhinge the seat belt and release my body from the back seat. I could feel the sadness of the silent tears that trickled down Susan's face and then dropped like tiny shards of glass onto her coat. Douglas jumped out of the car as I stood on the pavement to wave an awkward goodbye; he grasped my hand and shook it.

"It's not your fault Ralph; it's been like this for the last year. We lost our son, it's still incredibly raw, he was only seven. I try my best to keep going but Susan has given up, we are just going through life day by day, you weren't to know."

With that, he was gone but not before I looked into his eyes and saw the dark, dead stillness of despair staring back at me.

I made an attempt to window shop but within minutes I was bored and had retreated to the next best thing other than an alcohol fix, a caffeine fix. I don't know why I even tried; shopping always gave me the fear. When it came to buying something, I tended to treat it like a commando raid, in quickly without having to talk to any shop staff and then escape. Meg could shop for nothing in particular for hours on end. Thinking about it made me wonder why on earth God had bothered inventing both men and women. Surely it would have been easier for everyone if we had all been the same sex, preferably women though as I find men a bit ugly. I suppose the problem would be the human race dying out after one generation though. "Let's make children Hettie….ok, oh hang on Barbara I think we might have a problem."

Sitting on my own in one of the plastic seats I felt self-conscious without my phone to look at. It occurred to me that it felt less lonely being out in the woods than it did being in a coffee house without a mobile to look at and pretend I had endless texts to read. My age group used to talk about young people always looking at their phones but now we had finally caught up and become the same if not worse. The constant checking the phone to see if someone has sent or replied to a text; the excitement of a new message arriving followed by the disappointment when it turns out to be a reminder for a dental appointment. Relationships with friends were no longer measured by how often you met up with them; it was now how long since they had text you or how many kisses the message ended with.

The rain had finally stopped, and it began to dawn on me that as usual, I had charged headfirst into this trip without considering how I would get back. I had no idea where to find a bus, so decided to walk around and at least try to investigate the possibilities. In truth, I was beginning to miss Meg and the comfort of home, in fact, I was even missing Harvey. *To hell with a bus I will find a phone box, bound to be a taxi number pinned inside, get back early and join Harvey for a drink.* The problem was I along with every other human being in Britain had not actually used a phone box for years; I was not even sure if they took money anymore or if you had to use a phone card. We all lamented the loss of the phone box, the post office, the remote branch line train stations, and the local banks but did any of us use them? No chance, it's fucking raining outside, I will use my car, mobile and the internet thank you.

I soon found myself in the quiet suburbs of Dumfries having wondered about for an hour in a haze talking to myself. The streets were lined with those old-fashioned villas that would once have been home to doctors and solicitors. Now they looked unloved and most had probably been turned into rented apartments for students and lodgers. Just as the houses started to thin out I spotted a genuine old red telephone box covered in dead leaves and looking as though it had last been used in 1985. Prizing the door open I had little expectation of finding anything working inside and for once my pessimism proved to be right. The inside smelt like a garden compost heap and the glass was covered in mold giving a hazy green view of the outside world. The actual coin box was still attached although where the phone receiver should have been, there hung two loose wires. No doubt the receiver had long ago moved house to become the comedy possession of some students along with the traffic cone they had nicked on their last pub crawl. The interior glass was covered in crude graffiti and damp rotting cards advertising everything from gardeners to yoga classes. I found one for a taxi firm and took comfort in the fact that even if the phone had worked no doubt the number was so old the driver and his Austin Maestro would have long ago taken the road to the great scrap yard in the sky, or even better the one in Dalloway. Turning to escape the dank claustrophobia I pushed the door or what I thought was the door, but it was solid. Slight panic took hold as I turned to my right and tried again but nothing gave. I was certain the door had been at the front so with a rising sense of fear I tried the left side without any real expectation of it giving way and of course it remained firm against my push. The horror of being trapped in what felt like an upright coffin started to take over and I threw myself against the front with as much power as possible but still, nothing would give. *Calm down for fuck sake Ralph, this is ridiculous; you need to think your way out of this.* I took a deep breath and looked carefully at each side to try and identify hinges or something that would at least give me a clue where the exit must be.

It was in that moment of temporary calm that I sensed something approaching the box from outside. It was a sound that was familiar, and it was getting closer, tap, tap, tap/tap, tap, tap. With a growing feeling of horror and panic, I tried to rub the filthy glass to see outside. The condensation and grime only gave me a vague view, but it was enough for me to make out a bent, dark shadow clicking towards the telephone box about twenty meters away. It sounded like Maxime, but the shape was all wrong, this silhouette was haggard and broken like shuffling death. Blind panic kicked in and I flung myself against the front with every ounce of energy I could muster, it gave way instantly and I was sent flying out in a tumbling mess to land at the edge of the road.

Hands reached down to pull my sprawling body up from the tarmac. Two youngish men looked at me with drunken concern and amusement in their eyes." You ok pal, you scared the feckin crap out of us, I thought the wife had jumped out the feckin box you made such a scream." His pal laughed and made a good-hearted attempt to rub various dead leaves and dirt from my jacket. I could smell dope and then noticed one of the duo held a lit joint between his fingers.

"Here take a pull on that mate that'll sort you out", he said in a friendly Dumfrieshire drawl. I took up his offer while embarrassingly trying to claim that I suffered from claustrophobia and had panicked when the door of the phone box jammed shut. Rab and Colin proved to be two lovely guys and could not have been more helpful. Of course, after my acrobatics in the street, they assumed I was a fellow piss head, so I grasped the opportunity and asked if one of them could phone me a taxi. Before they headed off to continue drinking we shook hands and embraced each other at least five times, that never-ending goodbye that drunks do so well.

I sat in the back of the taxi and thought about what had happened while trying to work out why my life had ended up in such a mess. Meg did not deserve this; thank God the children had grown up and left so they would not have to witness my decline. Somehow, I understood that this would be the last crossroads in my life and the next decision would be the final one. Sadly, I also knew that unless the decision was made for me and taken out of my hands, I would make the wrong choice. The swerving of the taxi jolted me out of the self-centered melancholia and brought me back to the here and now. The driver threw the car into corners he obviously knew well but to the uninitiated passenger they just looked like exits into certain oblivion. I remembered that most taxi drivers drove like lunatics even back in Chelmsford; the difference was that in this taxi I was sober and not returning from the pub. Being drunk and heading into a wall was amusing, being stone cold sober and with my nerves still on edge was considerably less so.

Dusk had fallen as we made the last few miles back to Blackcraig in our Formula One taxi. I wondered what state Harvey would be in and hoped he would still be out enjoying himself. I needed a drink desperately as well as someone to talk to. My mind wondered back to Susan and Douglas and the hell they must have been through, having lost such a young child. What had happened, had it been an illness or something else? It was strange that we had come 400 miles to the middle of nowhere and ended up meeting such a tragic couple who lived relatively close to us back home. That last thought swirled around in my head, but why did it sit so uncomfortably on my shoulders? Why did I feel that somehow, I was meant to meet them? I looked out of the car window into the blackness and whispered to myself, "Christ, I need a drink."

## Winters Child 12/2017

Only a mother can know real love

Painted on her heart, carved on her soul

Only a mother can weep real tears

Etched on her face, wrought in her hands

And if you leave before my time

I shall count the years my winter's child, until again I see your face

And once more we shall merge our bodies

To become as one to never let go

# 5- The Silent Sentinel

I awoke early in the morning from a deep sleep feeling surprisingly good. I knew why, for once I did not have a hangover. Laying in the warm comfort of the bed I remembered back to last night. On arriving back in the village, I had wandered through all three bars in Kirkallen expecting at any minute to bump into my drinking companion but could find no sign of him. I had decided to stay in the last pub and ordered two pints of lager; the first one was gone before I took a breath to ask Carol behind the bar if my missing friend had been in. "I don't suppose you remember if a guy around my age, taller, probably wearing a wooly hat was in earlier?" It was, of course, a stupid question to ask as Carol was an attractive middle-aged blonde and you could rest assured that drink and a good-looking woman would have seen him camp there for the afternoon.

"Oh yes, I take it you are talking about Harvey?" she replied. "Absolutely lovely guy, left about an hour ago, he was pretty well gone though. I think he was here drinking all afternoon."

I half expected Carol to tell me they were getting married as she continued to sing his praises. "I take it you are Ralph, he mentioned going to another bar to meet you later. God what a laugh he is, he told me about the walk you two are doing." I was already downing my second pint as she continued.

"Harvey tells me you have never walked any hills before and he has had to help you along each day?"

I remembered suddenly feeling utterly exhausted and knew I had to get back to the flat and get some much-needed sleep. To my surprise, I had found a fully dressed Harvey deep in slumber laying on the couch in the main living room. It looked like he had indeed enjoyed the local hostelry in the village and then returned with half of it back to the flat. Two empty wine bottles and a half-empty one lay beside the couch along with his phone and what looked like the remains of a takeaway. I had managed to stir the slumbering wreck after some effort and convince him to go to his room and sleep, which he did but not before grabbing the last remnants of the wine bottle. My bones ached after a long day of walking and fighting imaginary demons, so I remembered deciding to run a hot bath but oddly on going into the bathroom I found the tub was already full of hot scolding water. The tap was still gushing more of the steaming liquid into the almost overflowing bath, so I had quickly turned it off. *It can't have been Harvey* I thought *so it must have been me when I first came in,* but I had no recollection of going anywhere near the bathroom. Another one of my memory lapses maybe or could it be Mr. Forests Ranger's mum wandering around from next door? The last thought had disturbed me more than the fear of losing my mental faculties, so I emptied the bath and took a shower instead before I at last hit the sack.

I was just about to get up and kick Harvey out of his bed when the bell rang followed by an impatient and loud bang on the door. I grabbed some clothes to go and find out who the anxious caller was just as another hard rap reverberated through the flat. *For fuck's sake calm down, I'm coming, I'm coming.* I unlocked the door and opened it; standing in the doorway was a large Scottish policeman. I don't know why but, the few times the police have spoken to me I have always ended up feeling guilty even though no crime has been committed. Once as a child, I was caught with a friend playing on a building site by the local bobby. For some reason when he asked for my address I burst into tears, mind you I was only sixteen at the time. No just kidding, I was probably about six. At the sight of me blubbing I reckon the poor constable took fright as he left quickly with a, "Be careful boys, building sites are not playgrounds." When I was a child the local police had that helpful laid-back attitude; nowadays two six-year-olds free on a building site would require am armed response team and at least two helicopters as back up before the police would move in.

Constable Morrison of Blackcraig could not have been politer, but he had that odd habit which bouncers at clubs have of not actually looking into your eyes when they address you. They speak while looking over your head at some invisible person standing behind you. I always assumed it was something they learned in training i.e. don't look directly into a person's eyes as they might burst into tears. Maybe it was because most Policemen and certainly most bouncers were taller than me and it was too much effort to look down. PC Morrison explained that it was nothing to be concerned about, but he required both of us to come to the police station within the next half an hour to help with an ongoing local enquiry. I got the distinct impression that this was more of an order than a request, so I asked for twenty minutes to give Harvey the kiss of life and we would be down.

As I closed the door my mind went into overdrive, what the hell had we done? I knew I had not urinated in the bothy, despite the temptation a few nights ago; maybe CCTV had picked me up smoking a joint with Rab and Colin after I somersaulted out of the phone box. To be honest I was finding it more amusing than anything else as other than being a pair of idiots we were incapable of doing any harm or damage. Maybe that was it, we were about to be arrested for being useless. It was Harvey's overreaction that gave me the reason to worry. He was already out of bed struggling into his clothes. "Who the hell was that, they nearly took the fucking door off!" When I told him, we needed to go down to the local cop shop his face went white and he staggered back to sit on his bed.

"What do they want, what is it, did they ask for me?" he stammered. He had the look of a guilty man, although guilty of what? Harvey did not seem to be capable of doing anything other than crack jokes and drink.

"They want to know why you were chatting up the sergeant's wife in the pub last night," I replied. "How the hell do I know what they want? In the name of God will you calm down, it's bound to be something daft. If you murdered your ex-girlfriend before we left Chelmsford then I doubt they would send PC Plod to ask us to nip down to the village police station."

Harvey's smile returned,

"Sorry Ralph, it's just the police always wind me up, I had a few problems when I was younger and it sort of still gets to me."

We finished getting ready and left to go and find out if Harvey was about to be locked up or not. I was beginning to realise something was not quite right about my walking buddy. I doubted it was anything bad, he just didn't seem to be that kind of person, but he was running from something; I suppose deep down I already knew that to be honest.

The police building looked like a film set from one of those homely Nineteen Fifties British movies. It was basically an old white townhouse with an office type frontage and an upper floor that looked as though it was used as a flat. We opened the door and crept in like a pair of criminals. Inside was a small standing area with a few seats, fronted by a desk. The walls were covered in posters with public information and pictures of missing people from various parts of Britain. I half expected to see Harvey's face staring out from one of the posters with the words, WANTED FOR BEING PERMANENTLY PISSED, written under his mug shot. Constable Morrison appeared and lifted the opening in the desk to allow us to come through. We entered the small office at the back to be greeted by a plainclothes policeman who was obviously a detective of some sorts. He introduced himself before telling us there was nothing to worry about while looking at Harvey's ashen face. *Christ*, I thought to myself, *remind me not to add him to the gang for the next great train robbery, he looks like a walking guilt trip.* "Are you alright sir, you look a bit pale?" asked the detective. I jumped in to rescue him before the cuffs went on.

"We got here early yesterday officer, I think my friend overindulged in the local hostelry to celebrate." The detective laughed and then started to throw questions at us without saying what the problem was, although it soon became apparent.

"Can you tell me exactly what time you arrived in Blackcraig yesterday?" "Where did you sleep the night before last?" "Did you meet anyone before you arrived in the village?"

It started to become clear that this was something to do with Maxime and eventually the detective got to the point on why he needed to speak to us. Maxime's body had been found close to John's Cross bothy by a forestry worker yesterday afternoon and his corpse had been brought back by the local mountain rescue team. I felt sadness at the thought of him dying alone up in the hills, but Harvey seemed to perk up as though it was a relief that this was not about something else. His good mood changed quickly when the detective explained that we would need to go to Dumfries to answer a few more questions.

"It's nothing to worry about, it's just that his death is unexplained at the moment and until they do a post-mortem we need to make absolutely sure everything is checked out. It looks like he died of a heart attack, unfortunately. It seems he may have been chased by something, possibly a wild animal had spooked him. Anyway, you are the last two people to see him alive, so you can understand why we need to follow this up."

"If you don't mind me asking" I replied, "How did you know we had actually met him?" I thought I could discern a faint smile on the detective's face.

"It's a small village sir, two walkers arriving this early in the year gets noticed by everyone, trust me. Oh, and there was another big clue, the body was found next to the hut you stayed in the night before last. We worked that bit out by reading the lovely comment you left in the bothy guest book Mr. Casellas."

The last sentence was delivered with more than a hint of sarcasm. Harvey looked at me sheepishly while I tried not to catch the eye of the detective in case he noticed my face getting redder. Then another picture formed in my mind that was unsettling, to say the least. It was Maxime standing terrified beside the hut while the apparition of a dead child shuffled towards him. What made it even more unnerving was the vision of Harvey standing watching, hidden in the trees as though he was conducting some grim act that was being played out.

It was agreed that Constable Morris or Calum, would take us to Dumfries at mid-day and then do the return journey later in the afternoon. Any thought of making headway on our walk today had been blown away. I was starting to realise that this whole trip was turning into a mess, three days in and we had barely covered 20 miles, less than half of what we had expected to do. As we sat back in the flat drinking coffee I told Harvey I was considering calling it a day and heading home. My companion surprised me with his keenness to carry on and complete the voyage. "Look, Ralph, what does it matter if we are behind some stupid schedule, we can blast it tomorrow and do 25 miles or even add a few days onto the end of the trek. The work won't care if we extend the holiday and your wife will probably fucking celebrate getting more time on her own without you."

It almost sounded like he was pleading with me, as though he could not face the thought of going home.

"Harvey, this whole fucking walk has been a disaster, we are not cut out for it, we seem to be lurching from one disaster to another. Come on mate, let's get into Dumfries, get the Maxime thing sorted out and get the hell out of this godforsaken place," I responded.

"Suit yourself Ralph" he replied," If you won't finish the walk with me I will complete it myself, you bloody wimp."

He sounded like a petulant child who was not getting his way, but I could see the hurt in his eyes and felt sorry for him. I just found it hard to understand why he would want to keep going.

I decided not to call Meg until after we had been to Dumfries, so I could tell her the whole story. Harvey tried another tactic to get me back onside as we waited for Calum to arrive and pick us up. "Come on Ralph, own up and tell them you nipped back and did old Maxime in with one of his walking sticks. Either that or he topped himself when he saw his accommodation for the night."

I could not bring myself to join in the banter though; it just seemed wrong knowing a person was dead even if we had only met him briefly. I was also finding it disconcerting that Harvey would act like a frightened rabbit one minute and the next he would be making wisecracks. Another human being had died and yet he acted as though it was just another page in his joke book. Well, it would not be my problem much longer; I could wave him off tomorrow while waiting for my taxi to Dumfries and the race back to relative sanity. Let him wander off into the hills on his own and drink himself to death if that's what he wanted.

The afternoon spent in Dumfries Police Station turned out to be an anticlimax. I had imagined fedora-clad detectives with cigarettes hanging from the side of their mouths, banging their fists on the table as they questioned us under a spotlight. Instead, we waited in a modern reception area for nearly two hours, before a seemingly disinterested plainclothes policeman asked us exactly the same questions we had answered in the village. With that, we were told we could go and as they had our names and addresses back home they would be in touch if further information was required. Harvey positively bounced out of the station seemingly back to his old self and still determined to try and convince me to continue tomorrow. As agreed we called Calum to pick us up but once again it was back to waiting as he informed us he would not be free for at least another hour. I convinced Harvey to go for a stroll around the town until our lift arrived. For once we both agreed that having a drink would be disrespectful to Calum, for some reason I had this picture of him breathalysing the two of us before being allowed back into the police car.

Spotting a small art gallery, we decided to go in and have a look around just to get out of the cold. While Harvey busied himself trying to find paintings of nude women, I walked over to look at a striking landscape painting of the Galloway coast hanging on one of the walls. A voice appeared from behind me, "That's a Frederick Macintyre, very famous local artist; it's one of his earlier pieces, quite exquisite do you not think?" Timothy the shop owner was a man around the same age as me and Harvey although that was where the similarity ended. He wore red trousers and a green woolen sweater with a silk scarf curled around his neck and obviously took time to think about what he would wear each morning. He was the sort of person who made comments like, *my wife is a lover of the arts, we met in Paris while perusing The Musee D'Orsay* or *I find Joyce's Ulysses to be more contemporary than modernist, would you not agree?*

As I was now cornered I had to say something and the obvious reply was, "Yes, it's a lovely painting, how much is it?" Timothy's eyes lit up,

"Well its nine hundred pounds but that includes the frame and if you are really interested I could maybe offer you a ten percent discount."

I could sense Harvey smirking in the background at the corner I had maneuvered myself into. "Yes, that seems very reasonable, maybe I will come back later and take another look after speaking to my wife." As soon as the words had left my mouth Timothy knew I was a time waster and we both understood that he was not going to sell me anything unless it cost less than fifty pence. He turned without replying and walked back over to the small counter to continue whatever he had been doing before I had walked in.

Harvey wondered over to me with a grin on his face, "Ok Picasso, shall we go and get a coffee, or do you want to call the wife and see if she has a spare nine hundred pounds in her purse?" I ignored his sarcasm though as something had caught my eye in the corner near the front window. A small picture was lying on its side with a few other paintings piled up against it. I picked the little frame up to have a look despite my companions, "Christ do you never learn," ringing in my ears. It was a small detailed pencil drawing of a young boy bending down prodding a stick into a puddle. His face was hidden as he looked down at the water, while his slightly older sister smiled with pride as she stood beside him. In the background was one of those thatched cottages you used to find all over the countryside in the south of England. I tried to re-engage with Timothy and he reluctantly sidled over to look at the picture.

"Yes, an old chap came in with it yesterday, it was Fi, my partner who spoke to him, I assume he was having a house clearance and wants to get what he can for it. The strange thing is it has no signature, so we have no way of knowing how to price it."

I put the painting down and made my way out; even though I could not see the boy's face his shape was identical to the one I imagined a few nights ago at the bothy.

We walked on without talking, maybe it was Maxime or the painting or something else but when I noticed a small church nearby I felt compelled to go in and have a look. Harvey declined to follow me and had a look on his face that said *weddings and funerals only mate*. It was a surprise to find the door open, maybe even the vandal's feared retribution in the afterlife. A mass of flickering candles gave a dim light around the altar at the front while a few faint light bulbs on the side walls added to the shadowy effect. A solitary figure of a black clad woman sat kneeling in the front row with her back to me, but other than that it was empty and silent. I took a pew at the edge of one of the middle rows and thought about Maxime and Susan, wondering why it was that only death could pull me into a church. The door opened quietly at the back and a rush of wind made the candles flicker violently around the pulpit. I assumed it was Harvey deciding to follow me after all but could not turn around to look. That same feeling of claustrophobia and fear that I had felt in the phone box started to creep up on me again. The silent woman kneeling in front seemed to hold my gaze as if in a vice, although I desperately wanted to see who was behind me. The candles continued to flicker as though caught in a storm as I held onto the front seat, frozen with fear in case they went out and I lost sight of the kneeling figure before me. *Get a grip Ralph, face your demons, this is crazy, you have nothing to fear but your own imagination.* I took a deep breath and stood up while keeping my gaze fixed firmly downward. Then calmly taking one measured step at a time I walked to the door and pushed it open to burst back out into the daylight. Of course, there was no sign of Harvey. The sudden coolness outside was a shock and I could feel the sweat on my t-shirt under the heavy walking coat, but I did not care. I felt relief, I felt alive. I had faced my demons and walked away. *Fuck them, I am not going crazy, you can beat this Ralph, none of this is real.*

Calum duly turned up and gave us a run back to Blackcraig, he drove just as fast as the taxi driver had the previous day and once again I was sober enough not to enjoy it. We headed straight into the Kenbridge hotel, if ever we needed a drink it was now. Knowing I was returning home tomorrow allowed me the excuse to let myself go and I felt I owed it to Harvey to have a last party with him. We spent the next few hours trying to convince each other of the merits of either going home or carrying on, neither of us willing to give ground. I simply could not understand Harvey even thinking of walking on alone, he was the most unenthusiastic, useless walker ever. Why not just go back to Chelmsford and get drunk, without the walking part getting in the way? I pleaded with him but the more he had to drink the more determined he became in his argument to see the trip out.

The pub was quiet except for a handful of people, so while Harvey tried to chat up the bar staff I stepped outside to call Meg. It was time to tell her the good news, I was coming home. The call to Chelmsford and the subsequent conversation did not go the way I had expected. Maybe it was her friend being so ill in hospital or the fact that I was drunk again but Meg sounded cold and unresponsive. I tried to explain what had happened and my reasons for calling it a day and heading back to Chelmsford. Of course, I left out the parts about see seeing ghosts as well as the amount of drinking we had been indulging in, but somehow, I could tell that she knew I was lying again.

"Ralph, I don't want you to come home, you have to finish the journey, there is no way back now." The words did not even sound like her, it was Meg's voice but as if spoken by another person. The ultimatum had arrived as it eventually had to I suppose. We both now understood I was walking in a dead man's shoes and that our relationship looked equally doomed. Her voice started to slowly fade as though static was washing over the airwaves.

"I don't know any more Ralph, I just can't go on like this, follow the path, it is our only chance." "I love you, Meg, I am truly sorry," I whispered back and thought I heard a faint goodbye crackle in response as though spoken by a stranger, and then the phone went silent. It was as if someone had reluctantly turned the last page of a book they had once loved but would never read again.

The look of relief on Harvey's face was a sight to behold. He grabbed me in a drunken embrace and nearly squeezed out what little life was left in me. Now I finally understood that this walk had always been my destiny and we were both here for a reason. As we continued to drink into the evening I pushed him harder for an explanation about the way he acted when the police had called and why was he not telling me what was going on." Look, Ralph," he replied, "I admit I am in a little bit of trouble with the police back home, it's nothing big but I need to stay away for a while, I got myself involved in something and just need time to allow things to settle down."

I could see in his eyes that he was lying though; they say you should look into someone's eyes to see the truth and his spoke of something far worse than needing time out. I would get the truth eventually; it was just a matter of waiting. The path would squeeze it out just as it had squeezed out the last breath from Maxime.

We continued drinking in the few local pubs the village offered us for the rest of the evening, becoming more and more passionate about finishing the walk as the beer flowed. It reminded me of being back in Chelmsford with the mates getting drunk and everyone getting increasingly excited at the thought of joining me. The only difference is that I would wake up in the morning with a rotten headache and without the option of texting to say, *sorry I got a bit carried away last night and you know I can't walk the length of myself; maybe one of your other friends will go.* Anyway, I was now in the same boat as Harvey, what was there to go home for? The path was our only way to salvation or damnation, it had been that way from the minute I had stepped out of the house in Chelmsford and the first cut of the wind had run through my bones. At some point, we ordered food in one of the small hotels and of course, that meant switching to wine. "Chardonnay, Riesling, Moscato?" I enquired of my companion while pretending to read the tiny blurred writing on the wine list.

"Just tell them two bottles of whatever is the cheapest and not to bother with that tasting nonsense they do. I want to drink the fucking stuff not look at it," replied my articulate friend. As the evening progressed the lounge became busier and I could see people looking over at us as we became louder.

"I think we should consider calling it a night Harvey before Constable Morrison arrives to turf us out. Anyway, I know you don't like the cops since you buried your ex in the back garden." Even in his inebriated state, I could see he managed a wry smile back to me. We staggered up the road but not before Harvey had successfully talked the barman into selling us a few bottles of wine to take home, as the local shop had shut for the night. I could tell that the hotel was not allowed to sell alcohol to take away, but the barman was not going to argue with a large drunk Englishman and upset the other diners. I glanced at his face as we shouted goodnight and could see the look of utter contempt he had for us. I imagined he was probably thinking about Scottish independence and praying for the day.

Before we had even walked back to the flat at the end of the village, Harvey decided to lower the tone even further. "I need a fucking pee Ralph, hang on for a minute old chap" and with that, he disappeared into the shadow cast by a large overhanging tree. While I waited, I admired its huge dark outline against the dimly lit street and the starlit sky. It looked like it had stood there for centuries but was now in decline; the wind and rain adding to the ravages of time to attack its once-towering glory. No doubt each year it would lose some of its nobbled branches onto the street below for the council to throw into the back of their van. Eventually, its noble attempt to match the young trees for greenery in the summer and the increasing habit of dropping bits onto the unsuspecting public below would lead to the final death sentence. Then the big lorry with the chainsaw would arrive to carry out the verdict. The next day, the old timer in the village would do his daily walk for the morning paper and wonder why things looked different. Two hundred years standing tall and proud watching over the village like a silent sentinel; forgotten in the blink of an eye.

We polished off the wine before retiring to our rooms for the night, utterly intoxicated. Even in my drunken state I knew we would have to make the effort to be up early in the morning to try and catch up on lost time. The next stage was a long unbroken hike through the extremely remote Galloway hills to the next tiny village at Kirkallan, a total of thirty-nine very lonely miles. We knew we would have to break open the tents and camp for the first time tomorrow as well. Of course, it all sounded perfectly reasonable after numerous bottles of wine, but even in our drunken state, we realised it was going to be hell. "Goodnight Harvey and remember, no mucking about. Up at six thirty and hit the track for seven. I am deadly serious this time," I shouted as he staggered towards his room.

"Goodnight Ralph old boy." He stopped and turned around with a worried look on his face. "Can I ask you just one last question old chap?" He sounded as though he expected a rejection.

"Yes, what is it Harvey?"

"Can I suggest we go to the shop before we leave in the morning and get some whisky to take with us? It would be bloody murder to camp outside in this cold without just a little drink." He looked at me hopefully waiting for a response.

"Good idea," I replied, "Let's have a lie in and be out for nine in case the shop is not open until then."

My drunken companion smiled back as though he had just hit the jackpot, "Yes three bottles of whisky and something to drink as well."

Leaving my friend to disappear into his room I headed off to use the bathroom. While standing at the toilet trying to keep from falling over, I smiled to myself at the day's events. Alcohol is an amazing thing; it just makes even the toughest of days seem good. That hazy drunk feeling when all is right with the world and you can view life from a distance as though watching from above. Why did they have to invent something that was so good and yet so bad for you? Why did it make you feel so alive while at the same time doing the exact opposite and slowly killing you? Suddenly I became aware that even though the heating was on the bathroom felt icy cold and then the stench hit me. The smell of death burned into my nostrils as I started to realise I was not alone, something was creeping into the edge of my vision. My body froze, every muscle tensed and locked up as though I was made of stone, and then reluctantly my head slowly turned as if being driven to look by some external force. Laying in the bath looking directly at me was the old man I had seen or thought I had seen on the train, the same one who had watched me from a distance in Carlisle. His hollow sunken eyes and long-dead face stared at me malevolently from the dead stagnant water that his decaying body floated in.

I stumbled in blind panic out of the bathroom not daring to look back, although I knew if I did the vision would most likely have gone. Cowering in my bed that night I cursed Harvey and my addiction, the same story being repeated over and over again. Tomorrow I would force the bastard to tell me what he was running from. Tomorrow I would break the cycle and stop drinking. I could not continue on like this with these horrors chasing me and haunting my brain. Yes, tomorrow would be the end; I would give up drinking forever. I would get back with Meg and remain sober for the rest of my life. Tomorrow, tomorrow, tomorrow. And of course, at that very moment, at that very point in time, I meant it, I really did.

The Silent Sentinel

Black Tree, Black Tree

Your heart so dark, watching waiting, no icy touch beyond
your reach

Changeling, Chameleon, so deep in despair, roots to search,
roots to dream

Wither and die to find relief, blend your deep winter with a
touch of life

Black Tree, Black Tree

Let the morning betray the night's cruel hold

To the dawn your hope, to the stars your soul

And let me know you see life in your gaze

Black Tree, Black Tree

Leave the despair and toil of your heart behind

To see passing strangers for what they are

For in us all comes fear of the light

# 6- Sacred Ground

The crisp frost crunched under our feet as we followed the riverside path to the edge of the village. The thin white coating of a late winter freeze covered everything, giving our surroundings a surreal look. It reminded me of one of those Christmas card scenes were everything blends together in perfect conformity. The local choir all standing happily singing together even though it is minus ten outside and the rest of the villagers are hiding behind their doors pretending they have gone to Barbados for the festivities.

It was barely nine in the morning and we were already on our way, shopping completed, and provisions stored in our cumbersome rucksacks. I felt different this morning and it seemed my companion felt the same way. For the first time on our trek, we had a reason to be putting ourselves through this torture. The walk was no longer a few days away in the wilderness to get drunk, it was now far more than that. We both knew we had to complete the journey to the end of the path and face our past in the hope it would give us a future. The only mystery that remained was what waited for us once we had finished, it could be the end or the beginning or maybe even both. Either way, it no longer mattered; the choice did not belong to us anymore. I knew I would tell Harvey about my hallucinations tonight as a bargaining tool to get him to come clean, on exactly why he had come on the trip and what he was really running from. Too much had happened, too many coincidences, even the death of Maxime seemed to involve us somehow.

We crossed a small wooden style and started to climb towards the summit of Waterside hill at five hundred and sixty-four feet. The low sun shone from a clear blue sky and yet it was freezing and would be unlikely to get above zero for the rest of the day. Despite yesterday's drinking I felt good and marched along with a purpose and a determination to complete at least twenty miles in the hope of getting halfway to our next hotel stop in the tiny hamlet of Kirkallan. We had called ahead and booked a room for the night after next, so we would have the goal of a hot bath and a warm room to drive us forward after a long uncomfortable night out in the cold. Within minutes of leaving Blackcraig, my phone signal flickered to zero, but I no longer cared. It dawned on me that the only person who would report me missing if something happened over the next three or four days would be Meg, and even that could no longer be guaranteed. Was that my imprint on the world after fifty-six years; the fact that I could fall into a frozen loch and only be discovered a week later when the one person left who possibly cared about me would wonder why I hadn't called?

The first half of the day involved trekking up and down various smaller hills as we headed towards the large manmade forest that surrounded the twelve hundred-foot Lower Benbrack. To the North stood the higher Galloway peaks, with some being over two and a half thousand feet. It should have been a bonus that we could only view the mountains from a distance as the path kept them at arm's length but even the small hills were hard going. Harvey had as usual fallen at least a half mile behind me. I imagined him shuffling along talking away to himself, the air blue with expletives. *Who the fuck builds a path that goes up and down mountains; this is insane, what the fuck is wrong with these people?* I looked in awe at the faint almost invisible track winding its way apologetically through the small valleys and hills, as if it was searching for the least tortuous route through the unforgiving landscape. It amazed me that this part of Scotland could be so lonely when it was so close to the border. Away to the South in the far distance over the Slowey Estuary lay the Lake District, just as spectacular but it could never have the loneliness and isolation that this part of Galloway held as its own. I remembered the grim warning in the guidebook that had seemed so amusing when we looked through it during one of our planning sessions back home or should that be drinking sessions. *Firstly, a warning. The stage from Blackcraig to Kirkallan is a very long one, crossing remote country through the Galloway hills, with few roads and no facilities save for a bothy at Grey Loning. Be sure to carry adequate food and drink.* At least we had followed the advice in the guide and sensibly grabbed a couple of bottles of scotch before starting out this morning.

It soon became frustrating having to constantly wait for Harvey to catch up just as I got into my walking rhythm. That's the thing about hill walking in this kind of terrain, even though you have someone with you and the scenery is stunning, all you really care about is putting one foot in front of the other by the least painful method possible. Life coaches would no doubt say; *it is the journey that counts not the destination.* They had obviously never walked the Southern Upland Way because if they had then they would have said; *fuck the journey get me to the destination.* I now understood why Maxime had become a walking robot; it was the only way to survive. Clear your head of everything but the motion of your legs and feet. Get into the zone and unless you are unlucky and meet a dead child, you will hopefully survive to get to the next stop or at least the next bottle of whisky.

I reached the edge of the forest at Lower Benbrack just after midday and waited for the lumbering expletive machine to come into view. Worryingly, even though I had a clear panorama back across the valley, there was no sign of my companion. Settling down to wait I lay on a patch of grass and placed my head on the rucksack to work out a plan that would maybe make the day easier for me, if not for Harvey. We had hoped to get through this large forest by four in the afternoon and camp at the edge of Loch Dee within sight of Grey Loning bothy. The decision to open up our small tents for the first time rather than stay in the hut had been an easy one. Surely nothing could be as cold and miserable as our night in John's Cross had been, and the death of Maxime felt like a warning to stay away from sleeping in another bothy. I continued to watch for any signs of Harvey in the distance and sat up as I spied the tiny outline of a figure some miles back heading along the track. But this was not a lone walker; someone was with him following close behind. *Who the hell could that be?* The last thing I needed right now was someone else to slow things up, or should I say someone else to slow Harvey up. *No wonder he was taking so long*, I thought to myself. I placed my head back down on the rucksack with an impatient sigh knowing I had a wait of at least an hour and started to drift off into an uncomfortable sleep.

"Christ, I thought you would have at least put the kettle on you lazy bastard." The shock of hearing Harvey's voice shook me violently from my sleep. He flung his rucksack down beside me in the grass. "I am fucking knackered; the guy who planned this track must have had a sick sense of humour. It's like a fucking roller coaster that only climbs up the way."

"Bloody hell you must have sprinted the last few miles, it feels like I have only been sleeping for five minutes, anyway who the hell was walking with you?" I replied with a hint of anger in my voice. Harvey looked back at me coldly, his eyes piercing through my head trying to read what I was saying. "What the fuck are you talking about Ralph, I was on my own."

I decided now was not the time to get into a heated discussion about me seeing things or about why he became so defensive and agitated at times. Maybe alcohol was making me crazy, but I was still sane enough to see the fear in his eyes again, fear that stopped him really pushing me for the truth, in case it forced him to admit to his own demons. I backtracked as quickly as possible to avoid any further suspicion.

"It's a joke Harvey; keep your fucking hair on. I thought you must have met someone, it's taking you so bloody long to catch up, that's all." He looked at me and then shrugged, both of us silently agreeing that it was best left alone, for now at least.

We opened the flask I had made before leaving and drank some lukewarm coffee. I was half expecting Harvey to suggest we top it up with whisky but to my disappointment, for once he said nothing. Maybe he was still drunk from last night or he was still pondering our recent discussion. I decided now was the perfect moment to tell him I planned to push on ahead to our camp for the night, so I could walk at my own pace and let him make his own way. "It also means I can find a place to camp and get things organized for you arriving," I said almost apologetically as though I was trying to do him a good turn.

"Sounds ok to me buddy," replied Harvey, "Just don't polish off any of that whisky until I get there, I know what you're like, it will be finished before you have got your rucksack off."

The joke broke the cold atmosphere and both of us smiled as we shook hands as though we were separating to head off to climb the unconquered North face of Everest in a deadly snowstorm, never to meet again.

"Take care big chap and unless one of us gets mauled by a grizzly I will see you in three or four hours."

The comment and the smiles were genuine, we had always been companions on this trek, but it was only now that we realised it. I turned and faced the imposing canopy of trees stretching as far as the eye could see. Soon I would be enveloped back into that silent world where the path could be seen clearly for once as it scraped its way apologetically through the black mass. I turned and shouted, "Get moving Harvey, your lazy big lump," but already he was hidden by the forest. It had already closed around and separated the two of us; as if it was reminding me that it was King of the Hills and I was only there on sufferance.

Without the worry of having to slow up for Harvey, I felt free at last and walked at a brisk pace. The forest seemed warmer as if giving shelter from the deep frost, but I knew this was an illusion as it was now below zero and dropping. The trees had an icy glow about them and faint wisps of steam could be seen rising off the tops as the low sun dared to fight the cold in the few places it could cast its rays. Both sides of the grassy track were hemmed in by an intense thicket of tall trees. I imagined it would take less than five minutes to become hopelessly lost and disorientated if you attempted to leave the path. At some points, the weak outline of the track would be hidden and then separate into other possible routes causing me mild consternation as I pondered over the map in the guidebook to see what direction the true way was. It felt strange having to make these decisions without my companion chipping in with advice. Somehow a homing instinct had kicked in on this walk, we had both commented on it, you just seemed to know which direction to go and it kept you from getting lost. So long as you did not attempt to leave the path and go through the trees then the day's destination would come to meet you, even if it was as the evening approached.

I reached the top edge of the large Clatteringshaws Loch; the water glistening in the sunlight. It felt good to have the company of something else other than trees for a change, although the forest still surrounded the loch as far as the eye could see. The route would follow the top of the lake for a few miles before heading back into the deep forest for the last five miles to Loch Dee and our camp for the night. It was time for another rest and a chance to finish the now cold coffee in my flask. I looked out onto the shimmering, deathly still mass of water, the low light of the late afternoon reflecting across the surface and wondered how far behind Harvey would be. It was hard not to feel a pang of guilt at having left him to his own devices, almost as though he was being punished for being too slow. It dawned on me that for the first time I had taken over as expedition leader and was now the one giving out the orders on what we should do. Strangely this new position made me feel responsible for my companion following behind me. The words following became stuck in my head...*following.... following*, shit, that was it, that was the feeling I had felt from the minute I had met Harvey at Chelmsford station. The sense that we were being followed, every step being shadowed by something, maybe not by a living being but at least by our past, our history. The voices in my head suddenly stopped their conversation as I sensed something happening to the motionless surface of the loch.

The still water had moved, just the smallest of ripples but it was enough to leave my nerves tingling. Logic told me it must be a fish, but my eyes would see what my brain wanted it to see. The hallucinations of the previous days could still not prepare me for whatever the next horror would be. I watched the water in frozen silence transfixed the same way I had been when watching the woman in the church. This time I would see my demons out, stare them in the face until I forced myself to accept they did not exist. The boy stood on the opposite shore half submerged in the water, his outline only just visible through the frozen mist rising off the Loch. The apparition's thin white arm was pointing, but not at me, he was pointing down the path, down the way I had come. Down the way Harvey would be coming.

I grabbed my bag and raced along the track as fast as my weary legs would take me, anything to get back into the all-encompassing trees and away from the water. When the boy and the old man appeared in the past I had always been drunk and by the morning they had seemed unreal; a figment of a diseased mind, ruined by alcohol. Now I was seeing them stone cold sober, I could feel the icy grip of dead hands touching my very soul. It had to be my mind playing with me but what if I was not imagining the visions? *This is ridiculous Ralph, get a grip of yourself; three months without a drink and you will look back and laugh at the state you got yourself into.* Anyway, I thought to myself, real or unreal what does it matter, a ghost can do you no harm unless you do it to yourself. The last thought comforted me, logic was kicking in again. We would get to the end of the journey and I could go home and try to sort my problems out, get my life back on track and get my brain focusing on reality again. The edge of Clatteringshaws Loch disappeared from view and I was back into the thick of the forest again. I turned and took a last look back at the still water and took comfort in the fact that it remained perfectly static under the frozen sky.

Pushing on through the trees, I kept a close eye for the vague outline of the track. It felt safer in the forest although maybe it was because I knew that the trees surrounding the twisting path kept everything from my vision, other than a few meters in front and behind. The feeling of being an intruder in an alien landscape was suddenly broken by the sight of a small wooden bridge across the Black Water of Dee burn. At least I knew I was on the right path as the little bridge was marked in the guidebook as a point to take a rest. It felt comforting to stand on something solid, something built by human hands and not fashioned by ghosts. The problem started immediately after the bridge when I arrived at what seemed to be a T junction in the path, one vague outline seemed to break away to the left and the other in the opposite direction to the right. The small guidebook was no help as the maps did not go into that kind of detail, but I found it strange that the text failed to mention anything about the track splitting in two. I had no idea which fork to take, so much for the homing instinct we had complimented each other about earlier in the day.

*What the hell*, I thought; *I will go right and can always turn back if the track peters out as it surely will do if it's the wrong way.* I was probably more annoyed at the thought of Harvey reaching the same point in an hour or so and picking the left path to arrive at the proposed camp site before me. No doubt he would be sitting in front of his already assembled tent roasting sausages on the fire with a smug grin across his face. *You must have taken the wrong turning Ralph, I should never have let you go on alone. Could you pass me back over the Captain's armband old chap, if you would be so kind?"* Now go and collect some firewood while I smoke my pipe and work out our route for tomorrow.

The right-hand track started to climb and almost immediately I began to feel I might have made the wrong choice. Surely, I should be descending to Loch Dee? However, I felt a compulsion to go on just in case. Rounding a bend in the trees I came upon a small clearing. I assumed it was part of a fire break opened up by the forestry commission to stop an inferno wiping out their investment. In the middle of the open space were the remains of what could have been a small house or even a bothy from many years ago. The walls had crumbled on three sides to stand only four or five feet high. Like most old derelict buildings, the end with the fireplace and remains of a chimney still stood taller than the rest. The place was surrounded with moss covered rocks that had fallen from the walls as the years took their toll. I decided to take a quick look around before heading back and came upon a strange site in the corner of the building. A small homemade wooden cross lay stuck at an angle on top of a grassy mound of earth. It had started to rot and fall over but still looked relatively new compared to the rest of the ruin, and I was sure it could not be more than a few years old. Any writing that had once been on the cross had long since faded but it was obviously a small grave of some sort; maybe it was the burial mound of a dog that had once been a much-loved pet. It was hard to imagine anyone coming this far to walk a dog but then I suppose bringing the remains to such a secluded location would have been the perfect act of remembrance.

As expected the path ended at the old building; I had no choice other than to backtrack and make my way to the junction to take the other turning. I calculated that despite this setback I would still be well ahead of Harvey and could make up the time if I pushed myself even harder. It's strange how you can walk over the same ground but in the opposite direction and recognize absolutely nothing. I had that illogical feeling in my head that this was not the same track but of course that was nonsense, there was only one way back. After about fifteen minutes I approached a bend that I thought I recognized and could hear the sound of running water. "Thank fuck," I said out loud to the trees, this had to be the Black Water of Dee burn with the junction near the bridge, and it was but, not in the way I had expected.

Standing facing me at the point where the paths split was a large German shepherd dog. It must have been at least ninety pounds and it stood transfixed looking at me, a low snarl emitting from its jaws as spittle and slaver dropped from its exposed teeth. Despite its enormous size, it looked emaciated and filthy as though it had been out in the wilds searching for something to eat for weeks. I knew that even if this was an apparition, it still looked real and that it was frightened and ready to attack, but not as frightened as I was, scared shitless would have been closer to the truth. I did that ridiculous thing most people try when under attack by a wild animal; I spoke to it in a soft friendly voice as though that would make it want to be my pal and maybe it would roll over and I could give it a tummy tickle. Not this fucking brute though, the minute I attempted to advance and cross to the right path it attacked. Sheer terror gripped me as it lunged snarling and spitting and sank its teeth into the arm of my jacket. I crashed to the ground with it still attached to me but luckily its jaws were mostly full of coat rather than me. The brutal power of the beast was enough to drag me along through the dirt and I somersaulted over causing the dog to lose grip as my rucksack crashed down on top of it. Luck was the last thing I would use to describe this bizarre situation but when it reattached its slobbering jaws to my backpack I knew I had a chance. Despite being dragged backwards I was able to undo the two buckles holding the pack and the whole ensemble released itself. The dog continued to try and destroy the bag while I stood up and in a moment of madness looked for something to attack it with. *For fuck sake, Ralph, leave the bag and get the hell out of it*, but for some reason, the dog had already let go and backed off snarling and slavering with its black teeth exposed facing me. I don't know why but I grabbed the bag and turned to flee back the way I had come, not stopping until I arrived back at the old building. Hiding behind the wall, I took off my heavy walking coat and gloves to survey the injuries to my arm. It was a relief to see that despite the mess the arm still had a hand and five fingers attached to it. The dog's teeth marks peppered my skin though and blood oozed down and dripped onto the damp grass below my feet. My heart raced as I strained to hear if the animal had followed me, but I knew it would still be standing guarding the bridge and blocking the path. Crumbling to the ground I hugged the wall and wept, not just because of the shock but because of my stupidity at having ever got involved in this hair-brained walk. *What a fucking idiot I am, what a total fucking idiot for ever getting involved in this godforsaken venture.*

With my other arm I dragged the rucksack from my back and tried to free up the small first aid kit that Meg had insisted I take. Of course, at the time I had complained that it would not be needed and just added unnecessary weight for me to carry but now I thanked her silently for once again being the only one in our marriage with any brains. Spreading some antiseptic ointment on my wound I watch transfixed as the white cream mixed in with the blood to become a grotesque pink colour. I could feel my heart pumping blood rapidly around my body as though my organs had gone into panic mode and even though it was freezing I felt hot and sticky. My attempt to wrap a bandage around the wound was laughable but it would have to do for now. I looked at my phone more in desperation than hope and cursed the fucking thing for having no signal as usual. Why was it phone companies could spend billions on making new models that could sing, dance and make the fucking tea but when you really needed it to do its proper job and make a fucking phone call it was useless. I knew why; it was because they made money from making endless new versions of the same phone, once you had bought it they could not care less whether the network allowed you to use it.

I started to feel nauseous from the shock and staggered over to the rear of the building to throw up. This was the first time I had looked at the back of the ruin and an unexpected sight greeted me. A small graveyard ran from the wall to the edge of the forest about twenty meters away. Most of the ancient memorial stones had fallen flat into the long grass, although a few still stood at acute angles as though ready to join their friends at any minute. The endless years of rain and wind had worn the headstones down so that any writing was only barely visible and almost impossible to read. It soon dawned on me that the building had once been a small place of worship; probably hundreds of years before the manmade forest had been planted. In fact, it was possible that a small hillside settlement had been here long ago, and this would have been the local place of worship and internment. Of course, I thought to myself, that must be why they had recently buried the dog or whatever it was inside the church, they would have known it was sacred ground. Then the unnerving realisation of the coincidence hit me. I had been attacked by a dog that looked as though it had risen from the dead. *Christ Ralph, get a fucking grip of yourself, this is crazy, or maybe it's just me that is going crazy.* None of this was helping as I tried to calm down and piece together what my next move needed to be. Reluctantly I concluded that my only hope of getting out of this mess was to go back to the junction and either arm myself for another attack or pray that the miserable beast had got bored and gone back from wherever the hell it had come from. Wincing in pain I struggled back into my rucksack and picked up a large rock with my good arm, but I knew I was done for if the creature was still there. Making as little noise as possible and taking small steps, I started on my way back down the track but was quickly brought to an abrupt halt by the sound of something approaching from the opposite direction. Dropping the rock, I turned and fled back to the sanctuary of the old church building although I doubted it would offer much protection from ninety pounds of rabid German shepherd. Shaking with both fear and the shock of my injuries, I cowered behind the wall to listen to the rustle of the path as it taunted me and directed its next visitation in my direction.

I don't know who got the biggest shock but the pure relief of seeing Harvey standing in the clearing will stick with me for the rest of my life. He looked aghast at the state of the terrified man crouching down behind the wall before him, "For fuck sake Ralph, what the hell happened to you? Your face is covered in blood?"

In near hysteria I stammered back, "I got attacked by a fucking great big dog, didn't see it back at the bridge?"

"A Dog? Are you sure it was a dog?" replied Harvey in an almost equally panic ridden tone. "No, it was a fucking

Rabbit!" I screamed back, "What the fuck do you think it was, I know what a fucking great big dog looks like, especially when it takes half of your arm away with it!"

"Well I must have come the same way you did, and I didn't see any big fucking dog Ralph." "For fuck sake Harvey, are you saying I imagined it? Look at the fucking bites on my arm!"

We calmed down while Harvey surveyed my injuries and then tied the bandage around my arm after washing it from his water bottle and putting more ointment on.

"I think you will be ok Ralph, it's not that bad once you wash the blood away, you might need a tetanus jag though."

"Thanks, Doctor Harvey" I replied, "Maybe we can nip down to the surgery and get a coffee while we are at it."

We both laughed, the fact that there were now two of us to face whatever the path could throw in our direction helped to calm me down.

"Jeez Ralph, I leave you for five minutes and you start a fight with a fucking dog. You did well to fend it off though, was it a Chihuahua?" joked my companion while he shook his head in mock disbelief. For a rare moment Harvey became serious.

"Ralph, I think we are in trouble, it's getting late and will be dark soon. Maybe we should camp here, keep cleaning your arm and hopefully by the morning that dog thing will have gone, and we can try to make civilization, or at least get a phone signal."

For some reason, it felt safer inside the confines of the crumbling sanctuary and I quickly agreed. Harvey tried to pull together our equipment but watching him was more stressful than trying to rest so I was soon up helping as much as I could. My arm felt painful but maybe Doctor Harvey was right, the injury was not as bad as it looked. Of course, if I ever got back home and Meg was still around I would tell her that I had survived a mauling and stared death in the face only for my companion to arrive and rescue me. On second thoughts, I would probably leave the being rescued by Harvey bit out though.

While Harvey tried to work out how to put the tents up, I quietly crept outside the ruin to look at the remains of the little graveyard. For some reason, most of us have a morbid fascination with reading the inscriptions on headstones. When I was with Meg it would almost become a competition to see who could find the saddest heading. "Meg, come and look at this one." *Julian McDonald, died 1846, aged three or Hettie Newbattle dearly missed mother of fourteen, died 1782 and so on.* I know it seems bad taste to even mention something like this but come on, admit it, you do it as well. Unfortunately, this graveyard offered no such enticement as the ancient engravings on the stones had all virtually faded away. There was one exception though. A little headstone was still standing at the very edge of the burial ground, almost nudging up to the encroaching forest. Kneeling to look at it, I read the words. *Milo McClenathan, dearly missed and forever in our hearts, Died aged seven.* The words then petered out as if washed away by the rain. And yet somehow this one headstone seemed different from the others; it was as though it had been prematurely aged to make it blend in. I shook my head sadly and walked back to help the now cursing Harvey who had made as little headway with the tents as I had expected.

As we pulled our camp together and passed the bottle of whisky to each other the feeling of drunken camaraderie started to take over. I knew the time had arrived to come clean with Harvey and tell him about my hallucinations and the concerns I had that my alcoholism was probably the cause. I also wanted to push him into giving me the real story about the trouble he had hinted he was having back home. Once I started talking, the pent-up emotion took over and I was aware that I probably sounded crazy. I hardly took a breath as I told him about the visions I had seen and the feeling of being followed. He stared at me without moving, a look of frozen horror etched on his face. I told him about the boy in the loch and near the hut as well as the old man in the bath.

"Why the hell did Maxime die and now a fucking crazy dog is attacking me…. What the hell is going on Harvey? This is just weird, it's not right."

I blurted out more than I expected to, but the release of tension just made it all pour out one sentence after another until it sounded less like a string of coincidences and more like an accusation against him, which of course, it was. I had expected Harvey to mock me and make a joke of it as though I was some hysterical teenager, but his response frightened me even more than the incident with the dog had. He was standing facing me with his eyes looking down at the ground, but tears were rolling down his cheeks and dripping onto the soft earth of the church floor.

"Oh God Ralph, it's not you they are following, it's me," he sobbed. "That's why I had to get away, I thought I had shaken them off, but I sort of knew something was wrong with you, I prayed it wasn't what I thought it might be, but now I know it fucking is. It's me they want Ralph, help me, please help me, oh Jesus please help me." As he spoke his voice trailed off until the final words were almost whispered. Then he fell to his knees like a completely broken man with his head looking down, so he would not have to look at me; In case I could see the shame written all over his face.

## Sacred Ground

We search through our lives for holy ground

To give us a reason, to give us a cause

We walk the earth like strangers to nature

To desecrate the soil, to leave our mark

The endless trek to find sacred land

While we kill and burn to claim our space

With toil and sweat to use up our years

And when we leave without the answer

Our dust will find a home in the hallowed ground.

# 7- The Confession

The after-work drinks ritual was in full flow at The Angel and for a Tuesday school night, this was impressive. It was nearing Christmas though so at least that gave some a reason to feel less guilty as well as an excuse for the lightweights to head home after only a few drinks. Harvey would always be one of the last to leave and often he would find himself having a solo drink just to round the night off before tapping the trusty taxi icon on his phone for the journey home. "Yes, of course, Mister Lindean we will send one round straight away, is it The Angel as usual?" It made Harvey feel good when Karen the taxi operator recognized his voice and ordered him a cab as though they were intimate friends.

"Yes, that's great Karen darling, thanks again."

"No problem Mr. Hamill, have a great Christmas when it comes."

"You too, and you can call me Harvey, Mister Hamill makes me sound like a school teacher", he joked. To Harvey's disappointment, she had already hung up and moved onto the next caller to sweet talk him into using her partner's taxi firm as well.

The taxi call would come later, as for now the booze was flowing and a fair number of the office were getting into the party mode. Calibar and Mitchell IT Consultants, employed about eighty people in their Norwich head office and Harvey was already halfway through a one-year temporary contract with them. The possibility of an extension loomed so long as he continued to dodge the bullets and let his colleagues do the work as well as take the flak. The recent move down south had not been greeted with any great enthusiasm by his girlfriend Sammy, especially after Harvey had made the usual empty promise and convinced her that the Manchester contract would last for at least three years. How could he have known that within a year the work would dry up, well that's what the company had told him. Harvey had a suspicion that they had simply found out how little work he was really doing. Anyway, what did it matter, Sammy had found a job in the local hospital and the way things were going he knew the relationship was probably heading in the same direction as all his previous ones. The fact was Harvey just loved to party, an evening spent in the pub was heaven after a boring day sitting at meetings listening to an endless procession of moaning while he continued to perfect the art of avoiding getting his name added to the list of follow up actions. The chair of the meeting would look around hopefully at the attendees, "That is a great idea Harvey, could I ask someone to take the action on that suggestion and report back to the meeting next week?" A prolonged silence would follow before Harvey would skillfully maneuver back in to play yet another trump card.

147

"Can I suggest Robert picks that one up? He is already working closely with the customer and has the tact and knowledge to hit the ground running."

It was as easy as that, job done, another bullet dodged by the work-shy Harvey. Meanwhile, his younger colleague Robert would be squirming in his seat, not sure if he had been complimented or done over like a turkey.

Carrie was considered by most of the older males as the office flirt, simply because she was in her late twenties, looked after her figure and liked to join the mostly male-dominated drinking group after work. If any of them had taken the time to evolve and leave behind their old-fashioned prejudices then they would have realised that she was simply doing the same as them, doing what she enjoyed and getting drunk after work. Anyway, she was single and if she could match her male colleagues in a challenging office environment then she could also take them on drink for drink. If truth be known Carrie thought of most of the guys as balding overweight middle-aged men who probably stayed out to avoid going home to their boring mundane family life. She did have a shine for Lester though but as always, the younger good-looking ones seemed to be either in a relationship or more interested in posing at the gym rather than going to the pub during the week.

Carrie was already getting tired of listening to her colleague Teresa babble on about the project she was working on. She feigned interest while scanning the crowded bar hoping to spot a chance to break away and move to another group, hopefully, one that was not talking about work. Harvey was laughing away with another two older co-workers; he always seemed to treat life as a joke, something to be endured in between having a drink. She liked Harvey, even though he was part of the balding middle-aged crew, there was something different about him. Of course, she knew what it was, he had never been married nor had children. He had never really grown up and so continued to treat life the way he always had, there to be enjoyed even if that meant you only considered yourself. The other older men seemed to carry an air of desperation on their shoulders, as if they knew they were over the hill but refused to accept it. Carrie edged over towards Harvey's group with the reluctant Teresa following in her shadow. "Hi Harvey, you old chancer. Any room for a couple of hot women to join the guys?" The joke was not lost on the three older males; while they eyed Carrie with drunken admiration they grudgingly accepted the middle-aged and rotund Teresa into the group. They all hoped she would not start on yet another boring tirade about about work and why she was the only one contributing to the current project.

"Well how could we possibly refuse the company of the gorgeous Carrie Darnell and her equally stunning accomplice Teresa Saunders, please do join us ladies," said the professional sweet talker Harvey.

"Ha-ha, don't give me that tosh you use on everyone else to get away with doing any actual work Harvey, it's me you are talking to remember," replied Carrie with a flirtatious wink back to her friend.

Drink was beginning to loosen the formalities and like most drunks, they had started to invade each other's personal territory. Carrie stood close to Harvey, occasionally their bodies making contact as they joked and laughed. The other two older males looked on with a hint of jealousy wishing they too could be a jovial smooth talker like their colleague. *How does he do it, I mean just look at him, that balding head with white curls dropping down from the sides and that pot belly.* The point they all seemed to miss was that Harvey had not only perfected the art of dodging work, he also had the ability to laugh women into bed. Maybe that was a bit of an exaggeration though. He rarely followed up on the bed part, even if it was laid on a plate for him; the problem was it would have got in the way of having a drink.

Harvey sat in the back of the taxi enjoying the warm fuzzy glow of the beer washing over him while reminiscing about his drunken flirting with Carrie. It was after nine o'clock and he knew things would not go well with Sammy when he got back. Often, she would be on shifts at the hospital when he tumbled out of the taxi and he could head to bed before the recriminations started. Only the previous weekend in a fit of remorse after a particularly long session with some of the boys, he had promised to mend his ways after Sammy had let fly at him. The sad thing was that in his own way he did love her, but he loved drinking more. Why could she not just accept that and let him be, it was not as though he was an alcoholic, just drank in the pub, but hardly ever in the house. Of course, the irony that he went to the pub at least six days a week would be lost on Harvey. The fact that he usually collapsed into bed in a drunken stupor meant he was barely capable of standing never mind having another drink.

On the few occasions Sammy was home when he arrived back she would have a go at him but then quickly give up. Harvey just simply did not react, drunk or sober he was the same, taking responsibility for anything other than his own self-gratification was not part of his make-up. Of course, he would apologise, try to make a joke of things and then promptly head off to bed after promising he would mend his ways. This time was different though and even in his inebriated state Harvey could sense that something had changed. He tried to make her laugh, even asking about her day and how things had gone cleaning up after the patients, but she remained quiet and said very little in response. In the morning he knew things had not improved when he turned over to cuddle up to Sammy and start the long process of trying to sweet talk her back round. The other half of the bed had not been slept in. Harvey staggered out of the duvet trying to shake the sleep away rather than any potential hangover. He drank far too often now for it to really impact him in the morning and after a shower and a coffee he was always ready for another boring day at the office, and then onto the real point of being alive, the pub. The note on the kitchen table was terse and to the point:

*Harvey. It is not easy to say this, but I am sure it will come as no surprise. I think our relationship has reached a conclusion and it will be best for both of us if we call it a day while we at least still like each other. You are a nice guy but will not accept you are an alcoholic and no pleading from me or attempting to change you is ever going to work, unless that is, you decide to change yourself. The first year in Manchester was fun but this last six months in Norwich have been miserable for me. I am moving back north to be with family and friends. I will move in with Brenda from work until I finish my contract at the hospital here, the sad thing is that you did not even notice most of my stuff was already gone when you came home last night. Anyway, I still have a few things to collect so will pop in this evening at seven after work to collect the rest of my gear and that way we don't have to meet up. I know I still have half the bills to pay for a few months so will keep in touch to make sure you get what is due, other than that please don't try to talk me round the way you usually do as this time my mind is finally made up. I hope you find what you are looking for in life even if it must be in the bottom of a bottle, Take care, Sammy.*

Harvey held the note in his hand, in a strange way he had been aware that this was coming but, in some ways, it still felt like a surprise. Of course, the signs had been there but somehow, he had expected more time before the axe fell once again. He was not sure if it was his ego that was dented, or he really cared about losing Sammy, after all this was not the first-time drink had seen off his relationships. He had always survived in the knowledge that some other poor woman would be ready and waiting to listen to his promises for at least a couple of years before she too would probably leave a note in the kitchen. This time did feel different though, the flat suddenly felt cold and empty without Sammy to give it life. She had even taken down all her pictures and ornaments so that the place looked like it had already been vacated and was waiting for new tenants to move in. It was as though the building was telling him to go as well, as though without Sammy it had no use for the guy who was always out, either working or drinking. For really the first time in his life Harvey felt lonely, somehow this did not feel the same as when his previous partners had walked out on him. After they had gone he had felt either relief or excitement at the thought of being able to start the adventure of another relationship. Maybe he was started to realise that there might not be many more opportunities. Even someone like him who could make women laugh would eventually run out of cards to play. He carefully folded the note over and placed it beside his car keys. Today would be different; he would drive to work and then come home at four o'clock and be waiting for Sammy. She would not expect him to be there, would not expect him to make such an effort and maybe, just maybe she would listen and give him another chance. He would show her he could change and that she could be more important than his other lover the bottle. And of course, at that very moment in his life, at that very point in the morning he meant it, he really did.

Mercy stood at the side of the road looking down with a mix of pride and impatience at her younger brother as he continued to prod the stick into the little puddle, "Milo, we need to go, come on stop messing around, mum will be waiting for us." The boy ignored her, totally caught up in the concentration required to scrape the short branch along the small pool as if the action would magically pop the missing ten pence out of the water. His search was driven not just by the determination to prove he could solve the problem but also to show that he did not have to take orders from his older sister. Mercy was used to this charade every time she agreed to take her sibling with her on the five hundred yards from the house to the village corner shop. Each time she would protest to her mum that Milo would take forever to make the short return journey and then both would give in when he flashed those cute blue eyes pleadingly while promised to hurry up back from the errand. Susan had let her twelve-year-old daughter take little Milo to the shop many times before although with it nearing six o'clock she did feel slightly more uncomfortable as the winter darkness had now descended. She convinced herself that it was irrational to worry considering the two children now walked to and from the local primary school each day. *After all, the village was fairly safe with streetlights covering the path and traffic usually slow due to the innumerable flashing thirty signs.* Somehow though, as she worked at the sink Susan found it difficult to shrug off that slight feeling of unease. The feeling that every parent goes through when they must let another little bit of their control go, another small step in allowing their children to grow.

The day dragged even more than usual for Harvey, and for once a few of his colleagues noticed his impatience when he was occasionally cornered at meetings and asked for a response. His mind was still working on what he was going to say to Sammy when he got home, and this sidetracked him away from his usual skill of being able to deflect any attention or project responsibility from hitting his shoulders. At lunch, Carrie strutted over to his table in the canteen with her other good-looking friend Emma. The arrival of the two young women perked Harvey up as well as adding another notch to his status in front of the rest of the guys including the two sitting at the table with him. "You guys going to the pub after work again tonight?" asked Carrie, "Because if you are then just try and keep us two away." Her friend Emma would not have been seen dead in The Angel after work, but she joined in with the good-natured banter.

"Ooh, maybe we can all go onto a club and dance the night away until six in the morning, just come straight into work afterwards."

They all laughed together as the jokes and innuendos flowed back and forth. Harvey amazed everyone by being first up from the table,

"I am going to head back to my desk as I need to get away early tonight."

Even this small act of responsibility was unusual for the man who refused to take anything seriously. Carrie looked at him with surprise as he picked up his tray and shuffled off to place it on the revolving shelf. She jumped up and followed him, placing her tray carefully to follow his into the netherworld behind the canteen front were plates disappeared to be recycled back out onto the tables by women in overalls and hats.

"You going to the pub at four after work today then lover boy?" said Carrie playfully. The comment about four o'clock took Harvey by surprise because even though the office worked flexi-time it was common practice for them all to work until five o'clock at least on a weekday. This allowed the professional drinkers to save up the hours owed and get away at two or three on the big party day at the end of the week. The obvious hint caught Harvey off guard and before he could think, the words had already tumbled out of his mouth.

"Yes, okay then gorgeous, catch you in The Angel at four, and it's your round."

Carrie flashed a smile back at him and headed away to flirt with the next old fool. She didn't fancy Harvey but there was something attractive about his ability to make her laugh, oh and the fact he was always up for a drink. Meanwhile, Harvey made his way back to his desk and tried to convince himself that he would have only one beer and then drive home to sort things out with Sammy.

Susan stood in the kitchen placing each dish methodically onto the plastic holder at the side of the basin. It was as if she was working on autopilot as she prepared the dinner for the children and Douglas, who would always arrive home at the agreed time. She had the demeanor of a woman who enjoyed her life; she doted on the youngsters as well as her husband. Douglas had always been the rock in her life, ever since they had first met as childhood sweethearts. Susan thought she heard the footsteps of the children coming in the front door but already that motherly sixth sense had set the first tiny alarm ringing in her head. "Mum", called Mercy from the hall as she walked towards the kitchen, the tone was more one of annoyance than any panic, but Susan was already sensing that something was wrong. She turned to face Mercy, her blood pressure rising in fear.

"Where is Milo?" The sharp tone in her voice immediately upset Mercy who with tears already forming in her eyes, replied in a frightened voice,

"He is just outside in the street, he won't come in, that's why I came to get you, it's not my fault, I kept telling him but he just ignores me!" Susan tried to calm her panic as she ran to the door, "Mercy, he is only seven, I have always told you never to leave him on his own outside!" Even as she burst through the front door and ran through the garden, she knew her life had already changed, and nothing would ever be the same again.

It was only five o'clock, but Harvey was starting to regret coming to The Angel. He knew that he would only get one chance to see Sammy to try and talk her round, now he wished he had headed home completely sober. Harvey had got to the pub as agreed at four o'clock, but Carrie had only just arrived and already others from the office were starting to show up. He knew that the main reason he and his younger colleague hit it off was that she liked to drink as much as he did. Despite his good intentions, it had been easy for Carrie to talk him into coming to the pub because he had been looking for an excuse to have a drink before he went to see Sammy. "Come on Harvey, I am really sorry for being late, that idiot Teresa collared me about some crap at work. You know what that bitch is like, let me get you another beer."

The temptation of Carrie and another drink proved difficult to resist although Harvey made a token effort.

"Ok gorgeous, but last one, I have to get home and I don't want to be pissing around trying to book a taxi when I made the effort to bring the car for once."

The clock behind the bar showed six o'clock as Harvey gulped down his fifth pint as quickly as possible and then making his apologies he raced outside to call a taxi. It would take at least an hour to get home and already he was panicking about missing Sammy. Feeling the car keys jangling in his pocket Harvey started to convince himself that he could drive home. *It will only take me forty-five minutes and if I use the back roads, there is no chance I will bump into the Police*, the perfectly logical voice in his head told him. *Anyway, I have always stuck to the rules and used a taxi after the pub, but this one time is different. I owe this to me and Sammy, this one little favour in my hour of need.* The voice was already talking to itself though, as Harvey needed no further convincing and was already steering the car gently out of the pub car park.

Carrie looked around the pub for her drinking partner, it was his round, but something told her he had already gone. She walked out to the back door just in time to see the headlights of a car slowly driving out of the car park. By the time Harvey was hammering through the never-ending bends on the country road, fear and guilt had started to kick in. He could not afford to get caught again; a third time in ten years would be serious stuff. Harvey wondered if three times could end up with a custodial sentence and pressed the accelerator to the floor; *get this fucking journey over as quickly as possible.*

Milo watched in delight as the ten pence piece flicked with a splash from the end of the stick and then rolled out into the road. He would show Mercy that he had been right all along and that the time spent rescuing the coin proved that boys were smarter than girls. His eyes focused on one thing only, the little silver coin that would be the trophy he would take proudly back into the house to show he was growing up, to show he was a man just like his dad. The blurred headlights of the car racing towards him remained invisible as they would do with any child who is caught in the moment.

It was nearly eight o'clock and Harvey sat with the engine switched off in the dark waiting for the lights in his apartment to go out to show that Sammy had collected her stuff and left. Beads of sweat ran down his face and his whole body was shaking either from the fright or the cold or maybe both. He had arrived back an hour ago and parked the car halfway down the street, so he could get out and survey the damage. The large dents in the wing proved that the sickening thud he had heard had indeed been something in the road. *What the hell had he hit*, he wondered when he ran his hand carefully over the edges of the smashed headlamp. Harvey had got back into the driver's seat and then looked in horror at the red stains on his fingers. *It had to be a dog, some sort of animal surely*, but even in his still half-drunk state, he knew that he could no longer go into the flat to see Sammy; in case she found out he had driven home. His survival instinct had kicked in and he planned to put the car into the garage under his apartment, so no one would know he had taken it to work that day. No one would be able to link him to whatever animal he had mown down while speeding through that little village. Lurking in the back of his mind was the stark terror and unthinkable fear that this could be worse, but his brain refused to let that chink of darkness into his world. That door remained firmly shut, for now at least.

Harvey survived the next few weeks by convincing himself that the awful accident was nothing to do with him. The police had a local witness who reported seeing a small green Fiesta racing through the village around the same time the young child had been killed. The media went into overdrive, firstly by focusing on the search for the car and then the tragedy of the family. Over the ensuing days, it would be Milo's grandfather Derek who would face the press with Douglas holding a crumbling Susan closely behind him. "I know it won't bring our little ray of sunshine back but please at least help us to get some closure and come forward to say what happened. The grief is destroying our family, someone must know something."

The pain was etched across Derek's face, his hollow eyes staring out with impenetrable sadness. Douglas would take over at the following press conferences but very quickly the media attention died down and switched to something else. The local press kept up the campaign and reported a month later that the police were still no nearer to finding the car involved, although the green Fiesta had now been ruled out of the search. By then Harvey was deliberately avoiding any news or talk on the subject, trying his best to convince himself that it was just a coincidence. *That green Fiesta must have gone through just after I did, it can't have been me. It must have been a dog I hit.*

At first, Harvey took to drinking at home each night when he got back from work rather than go to the pub and have to mix socially. Although he was still in denial that the child's death had been anything to do with him he still went through the motions of covering up any potential links that might place his car in Little Barling village that night. He waited a few months and then sold the old BMW for scrap, rather than have it repaired. He was also wise enough to drive it to a dealer nearly two hundred miles away in Brighton, just to make sure it would not raise any suspicion. The team at work including Carrie noticed he had taken a back seat from the drinking group and seemed more introverted than he usually was. When she asked her old drinking adversary what was wrong, he used the excuse that Sammy had left him, and he was missing her. Sitting in front of the television each evening Harvey would drink himself into oblivion before eventually staggering off to bed for a broken sleep full of distant nightmares. The media briefly resurrected the story after a few months to report that Milo's Grandfather Derek had passed away having never recovered from the shock of losing the little boy. A police spokesman stared out of the television with an accusing look that seemed to be directed at Harvey. *We will continue the search for the driver of that car, no matter how long it takes us. If you have any information, no matter how small it may seem, then please call us or go to your local police station.* The very next day Harvey called the employment agency to tell them he wanted a move out of the area and would take a contract anywhere they could find.

It was not the ideal move Harvey was looking for as it was only 80 miles away, but the agency convinced him that the Chelmsford job was a stepping stone to getting the relocation back to Manchester that he wanted. At least it was away from Norwich and a chance to wipe the slate clean and start again. Somehow Harvey knew that he had to break any contact he had with his ex-colleagues and friends. Cut any possible links and let the trail go cold. It proved to be the right decision at first as he soon settled back into his old ways and even managed to team up with another after-hours drinking group. In fact, if anything this lot seemed even wilder than the Norwich team had been. Unfortunately, there was no Carrie but for Harvey, another woman in his life was not on the priority list for now. He still harbored romantic thoughts that a move back to Manchester would be the catalyst for him and Sammy to renew their relationship. Of course, Harvey also knew it was the beer talking and the chances were less than remote; he had made no attempt to contact her and was now drinking harder and more often than ever.

Carrie sat with her feet curled up on the sofa and lifted the wine glass from the table. Since Harvey had left she had been frequenting the pub after work, less often. Somehow with him gone the rest of the crowd seemed boring. Anyway, she had also promised herself that she would cut back on the boozing and just have a few glasses of wine each evening and watch the television. Maybe even join the gym again and stop drinking altogether. While she considered this, she walked into the kitchen, dropped the empty wine bottle into the bin and retrieved another one from the fridge. In the background she could hear someone talking on the television, *if you have any information, no matter how small it may seem, then please call us or go to your local police station.* For some reason, she thought about Harvey, and then slowly something formed in her memory and the first seeds of suspicion floated into her brain.

It was only a few months into his new job when the first incident happened, and Harvey began to admit to himself that drink was beginning to impact not only his physical health but his mental stability as well. One evening while sitting in his flat with a bottle of whisky for company, the guilt that always lingered in the shadows started to creep back into his thoughts. He stood up from the chair briskly, hoping the sudden movement would shake the memories away and walked over to the window of the newly rented apartment. Harvey pulled an edge of the window blind up and peered out into the dark street below. Standing under the dimly lit street light he could make out the shape of a child who seemed to be looking up towards his flat. At first, the vision had little relevance; *probably just one of the youngsters who live in the street*, he thought to himself but by the time he had sat back down the realisation dawned on, *children that young did not stand outside alone in the dark*. He got back up, but the vision was gone. Over the next few weeks, Harvey would occasionally catch glimpses of the lone child either standing in the street or some other odd places, always in the dark and always alone. On returning home from work some nights he would occasionally get the feeling he was being followed. One evening he had turned around sharply and was sure he had seen the stooped bent figure of an old man in the distance watching him. Of course, all this happened when Harvey was drunk, it was Catch twenty-two; what came first the alcoholism or the visions? It frightened the hell out of him that he was starting to see things, but he would never admit to himself what was really tearing him apart. It was the slight chance, no matter how remote, that he was being haunted by something that knew what the truth was. Of course, the next day he would wake up and in the clear light of day laugh off the visions while telling himself, all I need to do is stay away from the drink for a while and everything will be fine.

Harvey knew that he should have stayed in Norwich until the chance to move back north came up and allowed him to leave the area altogether. The South of England now held the dark shadow of his past and he longed to get away completely and start all over again, almost as though he needed to clean his soul as well as his liver. The agency told him of a possible opening in Liverpool in a few months and advised him to hold off in Chelmsford until then. The chance to get away and rebuild his life gave Harvey a fresh impetus and a feeling of renewal. He decided for the first time in years to cut down on his alcohol intake and to look for opportunities for a week away somewhere, even if it was on his own. He surprised himself by for once actually following up with his plan and as he cut down on the drinking the visions started to become less often and eventually stopped altogether. Listening in on a conversation one day at work Harvey heard some colleagues discussing potential routes for a walking holiday. Of course, most of it had been idle chatter but he befriended Ralph who seemed intent on following through with the walking idea. A week in the wilds away from everything as well as the chance to forget his recent troubles seemed like the perfect tonic for Harvey. The two of them would head off to the pub after work in the weeks running up to the trek and over a few beers they would plan the trip. Hanging around with Ralph also helped Harvey slow down his drinking as although Ralph liked to drink he was not in Harvey's league, well not yet anyway. His new friend could seem standoffish at first, but Harvey worked hard to get him into his confidence and it felt good to have a friend. Since Sammy had left he had felt alone, even more so when the memory of that night crept back into his conscience. Harvey was gaining his old confidence back; *I shall enjoy this week in the wilderness and let myself go a little*, he thought to himself. Yes, the old Harvey was definitely riding back over the horizon with a bottle in each hand. And yet, no matter how hard he tried, the dark memory of that evening still cast a shadow that followed behind him. No matter how much it had faded or how far back it had fallen, it was still there, watching his every move.

## The Confession

Forgive me, father, for I have sinned

But it's you and your church who committed the greatest wrong

That you gave me guilt for everything in life

While you took the joy and held the trinkets

To keep your power, to keep your hold, while all shall suffer

Why should we have faith when you have none?

## 8- A Small Acorn

I could sense the dawn creeping into the silent world that surrounded the old ruin. It is that first hint of the morning when everything is still intensely dark from the winter night, but your eyes can still detect the slightest change in the blackness that surrounds you. The small tent seemed to wrap itself around me as though giving protection from whatever waited outside, whatever was watching us from the edge of the forest. The faint sound of Harvey breathing in his sleep could just be heard, coming from the tent next to mine. It was as though he was barely alive, unconsciously trying his best not to make a sound. Laying there in my sleeping bag, I felt the same. As if even the tiniest of noises would break the dead air and allow the ghosts to find us cowering in the sacred ground.

I had hardly slept all night as a multitude of thoughts and images raced through my head, to finally fit together like some bizarre jigsaw puzzle. We had talked long into the night in huddled whispers around the small fire, trying to make some sense of what was happening to us. With no phone signal, we had no way of getting any help unless we left our little sanctuary and faced whatever waited for us outside the ruins. Harvey had tried to make some logic of everything that had happened while looking at me with tearful pleading eyes, as though I had the magic solution to all his problems. And yet no matter which way we played it or whatever reasoning we tried to use to explain the events, it still came to the same awful conclusion. A child was dead because of Harvey and now we were being hunted down, as though the wheels of justice had failed so the ghosts would have their revenge instead. We agreed that drink could be impacting our thought processes, but it was impossible that the two of us would experience the same illusions and anyway far too many coincidences had been added to the equation, such as the death of Maxime and the dog attack. By the end of the evening we had agreed on one thing and on this point, there could be no going back. Once we reached civilization Harvey would hand himself into the police and end the family's long wait to finally get the closure they deserved. The only compromise was Harvey's desperate pleading to have at least a few more days' freedom and I reluctantly agreed we would wait until the end of the walk in Stranraer before we went together to the police. The fact was, I felt sorry for him, was that wrong after what he had done? The accident could have happened to anyone who was an alcoholic and had got caught up in a moment of weakness, that one mistake and your life is changed forever. The thing that was so unforgivable was Harvey leaving the family to suffer for so long and not facing up to the consequences of his actions. I knew he had simply tried to block it all out in the knowledge he would go to prison, and no doubt be branded a child killer. I did not mention to him about my encounter with Susan and Douglas the couple who had given me the lift to Dumfries, why add further horror to his predicament? Why add to his misery when I had already decided his fate was sealed, unless he gave up voluntarily, I would have to hand him over myself.

I crawled out of the tent and stood up to survey my surroundings as the first rays of daylight penetrated the trees and shone into the clearing. It was still cold, and the sky above looked angry as the dark clouds fought with each other for space. For now, the rain held back in abeyance as if waiting for the moment when the forest would reach out and touch the sky to welcome the deluge. The statuesque trees stood all around our small open space, graceful and beautiful but with a powerful malevolence like the massed ranks of an enormous army that had its victims hemmed in waiting for their final stand. The path had brought us all here to face the spirits of the forest and they had already passed judgment, all that remained was for the sentence to be carried out. I tried to understand why I had been dragged into all this and the conclusion seemed obvious. I had been picked to be Harvey's jailor, the one person alive who could force him to confess now that the ghosts had done their work. And yet the role chosen for me did not seem fair to my companion, surely, I was as guilty as he was? His life was no more a mess than mine, we had both chosen to drink our opportunities away and throw our lives down the drain. The only difference was that he had been caught; I was yet to commit the final act that would see my ghosts seek their revenge. However, I had made one decision as I stood staring into the abyss that cold early morning in the trees of Galloway, I would stop drinking forever. Maybe it was too late to repair the damage I had committed on my wife, my family, and my friends but it no longer mattered. What counted was that whatever I had to face in the next few days and whatever time I had left on this earth I would do it sober. And that very morning at that exact moment in my life, maybe for the first time ever, I really meant it.

Surveying the injury to my arm gave me some reassurance that I would hopefully be ok until we got to the village and sought some medical advice. The thick walking jacket had been my savior as it had stopped the dog from really getting its teeth into me; could it be that it had only been sent as a warning? The thought seemed preposterous but then this whole escapade felt more like a nightmare than reality. I retied the bandage on my arm while pondering our journey ahead. We had a massive hike of at least 25 miles to do if we hoped to make it to the sanctuary of Kirkallan before nightfall. The route would continue to take us through remote hills and valleys passing the edge of Loch Dee before following Loch Trool and a final twelve miles of yet more dense forest.

I opened the front of the tent Harvey was still sleeping in and felt nauseous as the stench of stale whisky made its escape into the cold air. We packed our rucksacks in silence; the feeling of equal companionship had changed to become uncomfortable and unbalanced. It made me feel like one of those bounty hunters in a cheap fifties cowboy film, tasked with bringing back the villain to face the gallows. Even though I did not want too, I now held all the cards and how much longer Harvey remained free was no longer his decision. He had become totally dependent on me, like a dog with sad frightened eyes that lives in fear of its one and only friend and master abandoning it. We each armed ourselves with a branch and headed cautiously back to the junction at the little bridge, but somehow, we sensed that the dog would be gone. It had done the job the path and the forest had demanded of it, it had forced the confession its masters required. "Ralph," His voice sounded weak as though he felt he no longer deserved to be heard,

"Even if the ghosts follow us to the end of the journey in Stranraer they cannot physically hurt us, I suppose they only exist because we let them?" There was a pause as he waited for me to reply and when the response did not come, his words sounded like a desperate plea rather than a question,

"What do you think Ralph?"

"Harvey, I don't know. I have the bite wounds on my arm; do you really think the dog that attacked me was normal? And what about Maxime, was it just a coincidence he died? I think that maybe our tormentors have had a hand in everything that's happened to us."

"Fuck Ralph, you are not making me feel any better. Oh Christ, what the hell am I going to do Ralph? What the fuck am I going to do!" His voice trailed off as his emotions took over.

I tried to reassure him, but he must have known I did not feel that way. The ghosts might be hunting Harvey down but somehow others had ended up being the innocent victims, but then everyone in this horrible tale had ended up being a victim, even the perpetrator of it all, my walking companion. "There is only one way to end this Harvey and you know it as well as I do," I replied

"Hand yourself in and admit your guilt, the ghosts will have finished what they set out to do. It's going to be tough, there is no getting away from it, but when you have done your time you can start again, without this shadow always following you. They won't give up Harvey, only you can make the decision to free yourself."

I wanted my words to help him, give some hope for the future but his silence told me otherwise. My speech had sounded more like a death sentence than a comfort. I knew he would be looking down at the ground, a broken man. Tears dripping into the grass to dissolve and disappear, just like the ones that Susan had wept every day since that fateful evening.

We made sure the little sanctuary was returned to the way we had found it before leaving and then headed out cautiously onto the track back down towards the bridge. As expected there was no sign of the dog and with a sigh of relief we continued onwards on our now silent journey. The pace was fast; even Harvey seemed to have found the extra strength required to eat up the miles. He walked with his head bent low, going through the motion like a man with no hope or future. Watching him reminded me of Maxime but without the walking sticks, the sound of his footsteps replacing the click of the walking poles. Putting one foot in front of the other for no reason other than to keep moving, to keep the beat going; *I am still alive, I am still alive; I am still alive, but only just*. We could sense the mass of water that was Loch Dee running close beside us, but the dense trees kept it from our view as we charged on. Just before the end of the forest and the climb across the exposed White hill, we passed a sign pointing to Grey Loning Bothy which lay on a detour of half a mile from the main path. The two of us walked past the notice as though it did not exist, making no comment or in Harvey's case without even looking up. The clouds overhead filled a dark angry sky and very soon the rain came down in torrents, driven on by the wind sweeping across the start of the exposed moor. Within minutes the water had already started to penetrate through my waterproofs to leave me shivering with the damp and cold. "How the hell can they call these useless fucking things waterproof," I shouted to Harvey, but my words became either lost in the wind or more likely ignored. As we left the trees behind, the western edge of Loch Dee came into sight. I stood for a few seconds to take in the view just as that familiar unearthly scream rendered the air to be followed by the baying of a dog, no doubt the same fucking beast that had tried to maul me. The first time we had heard it a few days back had been unsettling, now it felt hideous and threatening. "So, do you still think it's a fucking rabbit then Harvey?" I screamed hysterically, but this time I knew he definitely had not heard me. My companion was already running like a man possessed and was disappearing across the moor. I took to my heels and followed, somehow it felt that the further we got away from the forest and into the open space the better our chances. I was surprised at how quick my companion could move despite his size, but the irony was not lost on me as I knew he had been running from everything, all his life, including those who had suffered because of his selfish actions. It dawned on me that he had snared me as one of his endless victims as well and like a fool, I was letting him manipulate things, *why in God's name had I become part of his problem*? As we ran for our lives, I made my mind up that if we ever made it to Kirkallan the journey would end, and I would force Harvey to give himself up. *To hell with another three days of trying to survive while the ghosts of his past deeds hunt us down. Why should I have to suffer any longer because of him?*

We put as much distance as possible between us and the forest before collapsing side by side on the open moorland, completely exhausted. Neither of us could speak as we gasped for breath, I turned to look back at the trees half a mile away. The large black dog stood staring at us as though held back by the boundary of the conifers while in the shadows close by, the ghostly outline of the old man and the young child could just be made out. After a few minutes Harvey simply stood up and started walking again without having once looked back, it was as though he knew what he would see and could not face his shame. I hurried to catch up with him, "Harvey, Harvey, for fuck sake will you slow down and listen to me!" I shouted.

He stopped and turned to face me, no jokes, no smile just the look of a condemned man. The words spilled out from me in hysterical anger.

"This is fucking hopeless, if we survive the next forest and make it to the village then that's it Harvey, the end, it would be madness to go on after that. You have to promise me you will call it a day and hand yourself in, I am done with this, are you fucking listening to me, I am done running because of you!"

I had expected him to argue and beg for more time, but he looked resigned now to his fate. "Yes Ralph, you're right, I know it's not fair on you, just give me one last night of freedom and then in the morning I will go to the police." He looked sadly at me before adding, "Will you come with me Ralph when I hand myself over?"

Of course, it was not one last night he was asking for, it was one last chance to sink into the only comfort he had left and obliterate the outside world by drinking himself into an alcoholic stupor. How could I refuse a condemned man his last request, surely every person heading to the gallows was allowed one final wish? Even mass murderers had that one little piece of humanity granted to them before they went to meet their maker.

"Yes, okay Harvey, one last night", the tone of my voice sounding resigned and almost apologetic as if once again I was the one in the wrong.

We charged on but now in complete silence, the future was clearly mapped out, so words had become redundant. Up ahead the panorama of Loch Trool spread out before us, ominously the forest ran along both banks and covered every inch of the land as far as the eye could see. The rain drove into us so hard that I no longer cared what horror the trees might hold so long as we could get some protection from the wind and the cruel torrent that battered us. Approaching the edge of the forest I started to think about Meg and whether I would get to see her again to say sorry, to tell her I loved her, to tell her I was a changed man. The familiar sound of my feet crunching on small branches and ferns signaled we were about to enter the dense silent mass once again and I wondered to myself if we would be allowed to make it out to the other side. Stooping down I picked up a small acorn and placed it in my pocket, a small act of worship to the gods of the forest to ask for forgiveness and allow the path to maybe one day take me home.

For another twelve weary wet miles, we trudged with our heads bowed, saying nothing and without seeing another human being. Thankfully there was no more sight nor sound of the dog, but I could sense the ghosts floating in our tracks behind us, keeping their distance but, like the forest, watching our every move. Making sure that we stayed on the path and did not deviate from the route they had planned for us. Suddenly, I jumped in fright as the unexpected tone of my phone pierced the silence. The noise seemed alien because for the first time in days it was the sound of normality and civilization. I grabbed it desperately from my pocket, but my numb fingers failed to take hold and it went tumbling into the rain-soaked mud. *Bastard*, I stooped to pick it up but already the signal had faded, and I had missed my chance. I looked at the number hoping it was Meg, but it came up as *unknown*, even the word seemed to look back at me like a grim warning.

Dusk was beginning to fall as I estimated we had only a few miles to go until the relative safety of Kirkallan. The rain had at last stopped but it no longer mattered as every part of my body was wet and cold. I had been walking with my eyes focused on the ground trying to keep the rhythm of my legs going without having to think about it when suddenly I crashed into Harvey. He was standing, rock still, facing me like a human barricade, stopping me going any further. "For fuck sake, you frightened the shit out of me!" I shouted.

He was staring at me with a blank expression that looked both sinister and threatening. In his left hand he held one of the empty whisky bottles from the previous evening.

"The thing is Ralph; it's only you who knows what happened." The words sounded cold and hard as if spoken by someone else who had taken over my companion's voice.

"What exactly are you getting at Harvey?" I replied with growing anger.

"Why do I have to hand myself in? We could just go our separate ways, no one would need to know what happened unless of course, you decide to tell them, Ralph"

181

The tone of his voice made it clear that only one of us would be finishing the walk that evening.

The wind howled around the top of the trees as Harvey's bulk stood before me, his eyes staring into mine threateningly as though challenging me to respond. The tall conifers surrounded us like an expectant crowd at a boxing match, waiting with grim anticipation for the finale. I could sense they wanted blood, his blood. I kept my ground in silence and waiting for his next move, ready for the inevitable fight. I could have outrun him, but I was furious, I had never been so angry in all my life. I would make the bastard pay for what he had put me through, even though he would no doubt overpower me in the end. And then the standoff ended as quickly as it had begun when a loud tortured scream rendered the air. The realisation of what it was finally hit me like a brick.

"Listen to that Harvey; you know what it is don't you? It is never going to give up unless you do what it wants. Even if you kill me here right now, it's still going to come after you."

Already he was backing down, turning back into the Harvey I thought I knew, his face full of remorse and guilt.

"God I'm sorry Ralph, please don't give up on me, you are all I have. I am just scared to death, I don't want to go to prison, it will kill me. I am sorry Ralph, really sorry."

With that, he placed his hand on my shoulder and threw the empty bottle into the trees. Then he turned around and started walking again as though the confrontation had never happened. He knew what the scream was as well as I did, and that it would follow him until he gave the ghosts the retribution they needed. It was the scream of an innocent child as the headlights of a car plowed without thought towards it.

The lights of the small village of Kirkallan could be seen slowly approaching as the trees thinned out. I thanked whatever God had spared us as our feet finally landed on tarmac and we continued to walk up to the tiny hamlet in the dark. Passing what looked like a small restaurant with lights beaming out onto the road, we tiredly made our way up to the hotel. For once I was not disappointed as the rooms turned out to be fairly luxurious as well as being warm and modern, in fact, everything that the farmhouse and Marian had not been. And yet, I wished I could go back to just five days before, when my only worry had been how long until the next drink or how many bars I had on my electric fire. I wanted to return to being Harvey's friend rather than the person who would tie the noose around his neck. The stand-off in the forest had already been forgotten; somehow, I needed him as a friend as much as he needed me. The story would never have started and of course, it would never end unless both of us stuck together and played our part to the finish line.

Of course, the village did not have a resident doctor, but the hotel owner kindly offered to ask his daughter Hailey, a nurse, if she would have a look at the wound the dog had inflicted on my arm. True to his word within ten minutes there was a knock on the door. Hailey introduced herself and confirmed that there seemed to be no infection before advising me that I should go to Dumfries hospital in the morning and get it checked out. She looked at me as if trying to read my mind, almost as if she could tell that there was something different about the two walkers who had arrived in the village. "You need to report the dog attack to the police", she said, "I have lived here all my life and never heard of anything as weird as that happening."

The words came out almost like an accusation, as though it was my fault we had brought the evil spirits to her village and had personally insulted her home. I wanted to say sorry and tell her how right she was but thought better, it was obvious she was already suspicious and could tell I was holding most of the story back. I did not have to wait to triumphantly tell Harvey that we now had no choice but to end our journey tonight as I would need to go to the hospital in the morning, he was already standing behind Hailey waiting for me. I could tell he was afraid to leave me on my own, in case I took my twelve pieces of silver early and handed him in before his last drinking session tonight.

Hailey had confirmed that the only place open to eat at this time of year was the aptly named Glen Trool Diner in the village, so we walked down together but now in total silence. For the time of year, it was surprisingly busy with mostly couples or families enjoying an evening out in the little hamlet. The hustle and bustle of normality with people talking and laughing washed over the two hushed middle-aged men who sat together waiting to be served. Our relationship reminded me of those old couples you see sitting opposite each other in a restaurant and not speaking. It is as though the years have used up every available word and subject possible and it's sadly no longer worth the effort to repeat the same thing over again to each other. So, they stop talking and use the lonely grim silence as their last remaining bond.

I had expected Harvey to complain about my new-found sobriety, but he no longer seemed to care about anything, except drinking as much as possible. Watching him empty the glass down his throat made me understand why he came across as selfish and oblivious to the suffering of others. Was it really his fault, did the alcoholic really have a choice to be what they became or was it written from the day they were born? Maybe like all diseases some would be lucky and could be cured but for others it was terminal, and they had no choice. It was not that Harvey was oblivious to the feelings of others or did not care; I had seen how thoughtful and kind he could be. It was just that his body craved one thing over anything else and it would make him do whatever he had to

185

do to get that next drink. He hardly ate his dinner when it arrived and just carried on sinking endless glasses of wine. It dawned on me that I would have to stay close until I got him safely into his room that night, so the quicker he reached the stage of passing out the better. By the time he had finished his third bottle I managed to convince him we needed to go as I was exhausted and could see that even the indefatigable Harvey was close to passing out. Unfortunately, in the fifteen minutes it took us to pay the bill and walk back to the hotel he had recovered enough to demand we have a nightcap in the bar. After another hour and a further bottle, the hotel owner leaned over and whispered to me, "If you don't mind sir, I think it is time your friend went to his bed."

Harvey was at this point doing a fair impression of Anna back in Dalgowan and any minute now I expected him to come crashing off the bar stool. I helped him stagger haphazardly up to his room, bumping into walls and furniture on the way. Watching Harvey made me think back to the many times I had been like this back home and Meg had tried to guide me to my bed while I laughed at how funny I thought the whole thing was.

I turned to leave him as he stumbled over to fall onto the bed. "Ralph old boy, can I tell you something?" He mumbled, but at least the words came out in the right order.

"Yes, what is it, Harvey? Just don't tell me you have any more dark secrets, one set of ghouls chasing us is enough."

He cleared his throat and took a good few seconds to answer, the way most drunks do when they need to coordinate their brains and mouths together.

"You are the best Ralphy old boy, you stuck with me. Every other fucker gave up years ago, but you are still here old chap and that means a lot to me."

"Get some sleep Harvey," I replied, "Let's talk in the morning." He looked at me and just for a few seconds he sounded lucid, almost as though he was completely sober.

"I just want you to know that whatever tomorrow brings Ralph, no matter what it is, I forgive you."

I assumed he was talking about me going along him to the police in the morning, but the words sounded odd. "Ok Harvey, that is very kind of you, considering you wanted to beat me to death with a whisky bottle only a few hours ago, now get some sleep."

With my companion safely dumped unconscious on his bed, I was at last able to get my exhausted body back to my own room. That night I fell into the deepest sleep I had probably had in years. Maybe it was the lack of alcohol or simply from the exhausting day, but I knew the dark sleep really came because I could feel the weight of responsibility being lifted from me; knowing tomorrow all this would be

187

over and Harvey would for once own the consequences of his own actions.

The dreams started to come just as the first faint light of dawn trickled through the curtains, orange shapes flickering and dancing through my head like a kaleidoscopic picture show. I opened my eyes slowly, the room was bright but not with the subtle chink of light that heralds a new dawn, this was full of harsh black and gold shadows bouncing around every corner of the room. I staggered out of bed to open the curtains and find the source of the projections; the scene below that met my gaze quickly jolted the sleep from my brain. A few hundred yards down the road The Glen Trool Restaurant was ablaze, not just on fire but completely and utterly engulfed by flames. I grabbed my walking coat and stumbled down the stairs and out into the street to be met by a handful of other shocked residents standing to watch the burning spectacle. The hotel owner told me everything was ok; the fire brigade was on its way and it seemed the blaze had started up not long after the place had closed for the night. I looked at my watch; it was barely five in the morning. Someone behind me touched my shoulder causing me to turn around with a start. It was Hailey the nurse who had patched up my arm; she looked at me with fear in her eyes. We stared at each other for a few seconds; I could sense what was coming. "Why did you bring him here?" she said.

"What makes you think I had any choice in the matter, Hailey?" I whispered back. She took a step closer towards me, almost as if it was a threat.

"You started this, now you have to end it. You cannot walk away and leave this curse on our village, we do not deserve it. It is nothing to do with us." I could feel the chill driving into my bones as I faced the young woman.

"What is it you expect me to do?" I asked even though I knew the answer. I followed Hailey's eyes as they looked up at the hotel and then turned to gaze at the trees surrounding the buildings.

"Stop putting off what you know you have to do. It is him that they want, and we will all suffer if you do not end this, now. Do you really think he is going to go along quietly Ralph? For God's sake grow up and take responsibility and stop being a fucking coward. He is using you and you continue to go along with it like a sheep."

With that, she walked away leaving me feeling as worthless as I deserved. The blue flashing lights of a police car speeding towards the village suddenly brought me to my senses and I turned and ran back up the stairs. I knew Harvey's room would be unlocked and burst in to find the bed empty as expected and his bags gone. How could I have been such a fool, what a fucking idiot I had been! I hurried back to my

189

room to dress and throw my things together as quickly as possible.

The sound of another siren could be heard racing towards the inferno so before leaving I walked over to the window to look down at the ongoing spectacle. *Christ,* I thought to myself, *everywhere we have been on this walk we have caused carnage, you bastard Harvey, you fucking coward.* As I watched the street my eyes moved towards a dark corner at the side of the hotel. Even in the murkiness, it was easy to read the intentions of the figure as it stared with hatred in its dead eyes straight into the core of my soul. I had failed as always in the one thing I had to do, it had all been laid out on a plate by the forest, by the path, and by the ghosts and yet I had still screwed up. I stood transfixed looking down at the dead child as it pointed towards the west and resumption of the path and the last forty miles to Stranraer. I was being given one last chance, one more go to prove I was not a worthless human being. The malice that shone from the apparition made the consequences of not bringing the fugitive to justice only too clear. If I did not get this concluded, then I would be the next victim of his selfishness.

I threw only what was essential into my rucksack and left the rest in the room. The hotel owner looked at me in astonishment as I hurried down the stairs. "Just charge my card with whatever we owe," I said without flinching. I no longer cared about anything else other than the task I had been given to do. No doubt the proprietor would wonder why we had fled and might even link us with the fire, but it no longer mattered. The glow of the burning buildings guided me to the edge of the village and within minutes I was back on the path and in amongst the tall dark trees once again. The barely adequate torch gave me just enough light as I walked with a grim determination to make up the ground on my fleeing friend. Of course, he would expect me to follow him but what he would not know was that the spirits had set the fire to wake me early; now the hunt was truly on to bring Harvey home to face his sentence. I felt my fingers move instinctively into the pocket of my waterproof for the little acorn I had found the day before and then I clasped it tightly in the palm of my hand.

A Small Acorn

Through darkened sky comes bitter wind and rain

With my head bowed low and heart heavy with aching tired tread

But I walk with joy to face the storm

In my right hand a small acorn

As I see your shadow shimmer, dancing through the trees

It's then I know that I will always be home

# 9- Lost in the Ether

Carrie opened her eyes and tried to focus her thoughts to remember last night. It was getting harder each time to piece together what had happened once that evening's drinking session had started. Often, she would wake up with someone lying beside her and not be able to recall who he was, and even worse a few times she had woken up in a strange house and been forced to make a quick escape. The drinking was taking over her life and she knew it, so far, she had held onto her job and could still outpace most of her colleagues when it came to closing projects ahead of schedule. It was the increasing amount of days that Carrie was not actually making it into work that had become the problem; she had already been warned that any more requests for short notice holidays or sick days would be the last straw. Her manager had intimated he would take it further if she lost any more time as both her customers and colleagues had started to complain about Carrie not turning up at meetings. The fact that she could have covered the same work with a phone call or an email did not matter, if they had to suffer endless hours of sitting around a table going through pointless discussions then so did she. That was the law of the jungle on high-pressure project teams. Everyone was looking for someone else to blame, everyone tried to find a weakness in others, so they could exploit it. That way the fire could be kept from reaching their door. Some had been searching for a chink in Carrie's armour, she was too good at her job and that put them under pressure to perform as well. The murmurings about her drinking problem had already begun, too many had seen her drunken flirting in the pub after work and the jealous backlash was ready to start moving into first gear.

At least last night had not been a massive binge and she could remember coming home to her own bed and by herself. Anyway, today was going to be different, this was the day she would finally do what she had planned and get the monkey off her back. Her boss had listened with doubt in his eyes when Carrie had asked for another holiday, but he had no choice other than to support her. If he eventually had to go through the difficult process of firing his colleague, then the Human Resources department would investigate everything he had done to help his employee with a fine-tooth comb. He had reluctantly agreed she could have the day off to attend alcohol addiction counseling but wanted proof that she had really gone this time. *Anyway, that can wait until my appointment at two pm, first thing is the police station,* Carrie thought to herself as she poured a coffee and popped the painkillers out of the silver foil.

Carrie watched the police detective as he read over her statement, she could tell that a lecture was coming and sat patiently waiting for the inevitable reprimand. "Miss Darnell, I will get this information to the team investigating the Milo McClenathan case and we will let you know if anything comes from it." He paused and then after a few seconds looked up at her.

"You do understand that you should have come forward with this information twelve months ago, at the time of the incident?"

Carrie shuffled uncomfortably in her chair, she felt like standing up and telling him to go fuck himself, *that's the thanks you get for trying to be a good citizen*. She made him wait, as he had done with her before speaking.

"I realise that Constable," Carrie replied back sarcastically, "but put yourself in my shoes. I thought it might not mean anything and was worried about embarrassing an ex-colleague for no reason." The detective looked back at her, trying to hide the hint of a smile. It was hard not to admire the smart young woman sitting opposite him. Already she had twisted another old fool around her finger.

After she left he called the much-reduced investigation team that still worked on the Milo case. "Hi Mark, it is Steven at Bethel Street in Norwich. I think I might have something for you on the McClenathan case, something interesting. A lady called Carrie Darnell has just been in and says she worked with a man at Calibar and Mitchell in Norwich during the time of the boy's death. Now here is the good bit, it seems she was in the pub with him that night and he told her he was going to get a taxi home. After he left she went outside for a cigarette and saw him getting into his car, less than an hour before the accident. His name is Harvey Lindean and even more, interestingly she says he acted really strange after that evening and soon after took flight to work in another part of the country. Are you are enjoying this so far Mark? Well, it gets better. I checked up on this guy and he lost his license twice for drink driving some years back."

Carrie felt relieved at having at last followed up on her concern about Harvey. She had expected the police to give her a hard time about not coming forward earlier, so it was a good feeling to have the monkey off her back. Anyway, no doubt it would come to nothing and she would not have to see her old friend again unless of course, her suspicion turned out to be true. As she walked down the steps of the police building she thought back to that evening over a year ago. It was not the fact that Harvey had talked of leaving his car that night that had concerned her, it was the way her drinking buddy had acted immediately after and the fact that he had quit without even mentioning he was moving on. He had left the bar to go home and the next day returned as another person, cold and unfriendly as if everything she had admired in him had disappeared. *Well fuck him*, Carrie thought to herself as she turned into the street and headed towards The White Rose, he was just another waste of space like all men. Only an hour to go her appointment at the clinic, Carrie smiled to herself as she walked up to the bar and ordered the first drink of the day.

Daylight was breaking around me as I walked with a steady determined pace. The first few miles after leaving the village was a gradual climb to the summit of Glenvernoch fell on open moorland, giving clear views of the spectacular surrounding scenery. To the north, I could see Loch Ochiltree shimmering in the faint sunlight while some miles ahead the dark outline of the trees stood ready to embrace me once again. I could sense they had already closed around Harvey and now waited with impatience for the hunter to catch up. The forest would take me to the handful of scattered buildings that made up the village of Rowe. I would then dissect the B7027 before starting the climb to Craig Airie Ridge and the edge of Loch Derry. The Loch would be the half-way point of an 18-mile trek to the next large settlement at New Luce. I was sure I could catch up with Harvey long before then, although it was depressing being able to see the empty miles ahead to the start of the forest with no sign of my fleeing companion.

Suddenly my phone signal sparked into life as I clambered up to the summit of the hill. Clicking impatiently through my contacts I pressed the icon bearing Harvey's picture. To my surprise, it started to ring at the other end but then almost immediately went dead, as though the recipient had deliberately switched his phone off. I imagined him turning around to look back in the direction I was following, smiling to himself because once again he had guessed correctly. He knew I would follow him rather than take the easy option and go to the Police. I had no choice of course; this was about both of us, not just Harvey. The path would not allow me to walk away, I was guilty as well. This was between me and him now, there would be no winner, but it was still possible that there might be only one loser. I put the phone back into my pocket and having completed the climb, I started the easier and faster descent towards the waiting trees.

The two detectives sat silently in the car enjoying a coffee as well as the sandwiches that had been expensively supplied by the service area just north of Penrith on the M6. Neither Mark nor his colleague Nerrisa had heard of Kirkallan although they had a vague knowledge of the Dumfries and Galloway area. Mark had driven this was many years before while working on the case of a missing local Norwich man who had been sighted in the town of Kirkudbright, but unfortunately, the visit had turned out to be a waste of time. He desperately hoped that this lead would not go the same way and end in yet another disappointment. The Milo case had affected them both deeply; the frustration of a year following dead-end leads and having to face the torment of the family had worn them all down. The investigation team had diminished to just three officers and any day now they had expected to be told that the case would be put on hold unless something new came up. The latest lead was a major breakthrough and the two of them were almost afraid to discuss it as though by doing so they might jinx what looked like the longed-for missing jigsaw piece. Mark could feel it in his bones; he had been on the force for almost twenty-five years and could sense when that final bit of information finally arrived, and everything clicked into place. They had tracked Harvey Lindean's moves on the night of the accident and his suspicious actions in the weeks afterward. But the real breakthrough had come when they traced his car to a breakers yard in Brighton. The words the scrap dealer had said still reverberated in Mark's head, *yes officer, I checked back on our computer logging system and I remember the car and the guy well. It was unusual because I thought the vehicle was too good to put in the crusher, but he insisted and was willing to pay over the odds to get it done.* Mark remembered looking at Nerrisa and both breaking into a smile. Of course, the fact that the car no longer existed was a disappointment but at least it gave them something solid to follow up on at last. For now, the priority would be to find the two hikers and bring them in for questioning. This should be easy as it seemed they had already been involved in an incident and were known to the Dumfries police. A team was already being mobilized in the village they had last been seen in, and the two English officers hoped to arrive and find Harvey Lindean already in custody.

I increased my pace as much as my weary body would allow and descended Glenvernoch fell to arrive at the edge of the forest within a few hours. The trees no longer felt threatening as if both parties understood each other's position in the unfolding story. Maybe that's when life becomes easy, that point where you no longer care what happens to your physical being and every atom of your person is focused on the same thing. Even the voices in your head go silent; now they all have a common goal so there is no longer any need for your brain to tell your body what it should be doing. It was as simple as this, I would catch Harvey and force him to do what was required or I would die trying. Just before the trees broke out I came across a mobile phone lying in the middle of the grassy track. It had been deliberately smashed on a rock and then placed in a position where I would find it. I knew he was not taunting me, this was simply a marker placed by Harvey to make sure I would follow him. It was likely he had placed the phone just after my call, so it was not hard to surmise that he was now only a few hours ahead of me rather than the five or six hours he would be expecting. I knew

Harvey would continue his flight for the full thirty miles to the end of the path near Stranraer even if he had to walk through the night. I would keep going until he could feel my presence closing in on him, only one thing mattered now and that was the conclusion of our journey.

He walked as fast as possible although even in his inebriated state Harvey knew he was losing time as he occasionally staggered to the side of the path and either bumped into a tree or nearly lost his footing in the soft damp earth. The whisky bottle was already half empty, *why the fuck did I not get more yesterday,* he taunted himself. Only the drink would keep the demons in his thoughts at bay, keep them silent, keep them hidden so they could not torment him. But they would always break through, eating their way into his brain, accusing him of throwing his life away, ruining it for everyone. The psychological battle in his head would repeat itself each day as he tried to convince himself that he was the victim and not the other way around. Was it his fault he came from a broken marriage and an alcoholic father? The only person who had ever loved him was his mother and she had been taken as fate played its final cruel card on him. He had held her hand in the hospice when he was only fifteen, still a child. And from that point on Harvey had played life the only way he knew how. Play it safe, never commit to anything or anybody and that way you survive. Just laugh and drink, drink and laugh, drink, drink, drink…He missed his mother, he sort of missed Sammy as well but he missed his mother more than anything. The only person he had left who cared now was Ralph… *He will follow me to the end of the path, I know he will.*

Harvey descended from the trees to cross the B road at the little hamlet of Rowe and was already starting to climb back into the forest on the opposite side when the noise of tyres crunching on dead leaves and bracken forced him to turn around. Down below he could make out three vehicles, two land rovers, and a marked police car. He watched as the occupants spilled out, all except two of them dressed in professional hiking gear. It was obvious to Harvey that it was a search party and the person they had come to find was him. It was not the fact that both the dead and the living now hunted him that finally broke his spirit, it was the knowledge that the only person he had left in the world that he counted on as a true friend had betrayed him. "I thought you had more guts than that Ralph, you fucking little creep", he spat the words out to the trees in anger.

"We could have finished the trek, you would have caught me at the end, but we could have done it, you spineless bastard."

Harvey took his rucksack off and in a rage flung everything except the nearly empty whisky bottle as far into the trees as possible before taking to his heels. He would run, no one would stop him making it to the end, he would die first.

Carrie could feel herself swaying on the barstool as the afternoon turned into evening. Her companion had gone to the bathroom promising he would return so the two of them could go back to his place. Now that she had started to make the move to get off the wooden stool she realised just how drunk she was, and a feeling of nausea was beginning to well up in her throat. *Well, after all,* she thought to herself, *it's not every day you hand in an ex-colleague to the police and fuck it, I don't need alcohol counseling. I can stop tomorrow, no problem. I will tell that little weasel manager to go fuck himself. He will be the one groveling for me to stay when I finish the project in a blaze of glory and walk out into a new job.* She mouthed a last angry drunken insult, "*Stupid fucking manager prick*," before stumbling off the barstool and staggering haphazardly towards the female toilets. The early evening office drinkers holding their first beer of the day watched Carrie with embarrassment while conveniently forgetting that they had often been in the same state. Within seconds of reaching the cubicle, she was throwing up the countless pints of lager she had gorged on all afternoon. The remnants trickled down her chin as she knelt crouched over the basin and then ran onto the front of her dress. She remembered back to ten years before when as a bright-eyed young woman, she had been getting ready to leave home and go to university. Her best friend Olivia had always been around to come to the rescue and take her home after, yet another drinking session had gone too far. The cool sultry blue-eyed vivacious Olivia who could drink any man under the table and still smooth talk her way through whatever obstacles life threw in her path. How ironic that Carrie was now the successful one, she had left the little town to finish her degree and could pick and choose from an endless list of suitors if she wanted to. How sad that the tall confident and once beautiful Olivia was stuck in a council house with three kids, an ex-husband and was slowly drinking herself to death. *Every dog has its day*, Carrie thought with a sense of drunken pride. *No one expected me to be the one to make it; they all thought the great Olivia would be a roaring fucking success rather than me. Well fuck them all, I don't need any of them.* She started to wretch and was sick again while out in the bar her new companion looked around wondering where the hell she had gone. Meanwhile, the drinkers surrounding him nudged each other in sympathy as well as amusement.

As I approached the tarmacked road that bisected the forest the sound of distant voices floated through the trees towards me. Keeping far enough back to stay concealed I looked down onto the road and the few houses that comprised the settlement of Rowe. Somehow, I knew it was going to be people searching for us, so it came as no surprise to see three vehicles and what looked to be a mountain rescue team as well as a couple of police officers. What was unexpected was that they seemed to be assuming that Harvey had not reached the road yet and they were preparing to come back towards me. I headed off into the trees with a plan to find my way down to the road and back through the forest on the other side, hopefully, to rejoin the path at some point while keeping out of sight of the posse. Of course, in theory, this sounded easy, but it was not long before I was cursing as yet another branch struck me in the face. At points, I was forced to crawl in the damp thicket underneath the trees before finally tumbling into a drain that ran alongside the road. The water came up almost to my knees but at least I was out of sight of the search team. Just as I was about to run across the road I heard the sound of a car approaching and was forced to crouch down in the freezing boggy water. It was another police van but this one had the ominous words POLICE DOG HANDLER emblazoned on the side, the game was up, and I knew it. The van disappeared round the bend to join the others and gave me the chance to run to the opposite side of the road. Like a man possessed I flung myself through the thick mass of tree growth and battled on hoping to find the path again. I could sense the track was close and just before making the final push my eyes spotted the discarded rucksack laying on the boundary of the forest. I knew it was Harvey's; it felt like I had watched it for an eternity as it bounced away on his back to the sound of endless moaning and curses. Bending down to look at it the realisation dawned that he could now only be fifteen minutes ahead of me. Surely, he would have thrown the rucksack away on seeing or hearing the cars arrive. I also knew that he would believe I had turned him in, taken my thirty pieces of silver and betrayed him. The last thought was the hardest to take, surely the only reason the path had brought us together had been for me to convince Harvey to volunteer to face justice once we reached the end. Maybe it no longer mattered but I had to catch him first, let him know I had kept my part of the bargain. I dumped the rest of my kit beside his in the trees and burst out onto the path to run as fast as possible, using every last ounce of energy my body could muster.

The two forestry workers looked on with a mixture of nervous caution and amazement at the burly middle-aged man lumbering towards them holding a bottle of whisky. To see a hiker at this time of year was unusual but to see a walker without a rucksack and any other equipment was downright bizarre. They could tell Harvey was drunk and, in a mess, so they watched him carefully as he approached. "You can't go this way pal; the rainfall has brought some trees down and caused a landslide into Loch Derry half a mile ahead. It's far too dangerous mate, we have just been to assess the damage, can't see this being repaired for a few months at least. Paths closed mate, paths clos....", the two men looked on in surprise as Harvey ignored them and without looking or breaking his stride he simply stumbled passed while taking another slug out of the whisky bottle. As they watched his shape disappear around the corner to vanish into the trees one of the men took out his phone to call the police, only to discover that as usual there was no fucking phone signal.

Harvey surveyed the scene before him trying to rationalize what he saw despite the hazy clouds of alcohol numbing his reasoning and clouding his brain. The path skirted the steep tree-lined hill on one side and on the other was a sheer drop of a few hundred feet into the depths of Loch Dee below. What would normally be a pleasant if slightly scary walk had now been turned into an insurmountable obstacle course. The heavy rain that had fallen over the last few weeks had caused about a dozen trees to tumble down across the path and had obliterated the track into a muddy mass of broken roots and branches. Water cascaded down from the top of the hill and ran in angry floods through the mayhem of tangled wood. There was no logical way around the blockage other than to turn back and find another route. However, Harvey had long ago discarded logic and taking a last swig from the almost empty whisky bottle he turned and flung it into the mass of water down below and watched as it smashed off a tree before descending in shards of glass into the murky depths. He started to edge his way across but within minutes the realisation that he faced certain death started to dawn on him. With a resounding crash, his feet gave way from beneath and he slid into the seething mass of wet mud and broken trees. For a moment at least, the alcohol cloud numbing his body cleared and his brain suddenly had the chance to scream, *I don't want to die, not yet, it is too soon.* Harvey grabbed the nearest branch and made a desperate attempt to regain his footing. The only way out of this mess was to try and go back the way he had come. *Fuck it, get a grip Harvey, what the hell are you doing to yourself?* But as he twisted his body round to find a way out he froze in horror at the vision of the boy staring at him from the path he had just left. The black eyes pierced out from the hollow sunken skin with an intense hatred that bore deep into Harvey's soul. It was as if the ghost had rotted into a decaying mess for the last year as it waited for the justice that only he could give it. Even though he was twenty yards away from the horrible vision Harvey could smell the stagnant flesh that hung from its body. He turned in a blind panic and continued the impossible task of trying to get over the broken trees but already he could feel his feet giving way again as he collapsed into the mud and held on desperately to the same branch. How ironic that part of a dead tree was now the only thing that held him from joining the spirits and sliding down into the black emptiness of the water below.

The two forestry workers looked with wearied amusement at me as I approached. "Is this some kind of joke?" the younger looking one said.

"Got to be fucking Jeremy Beadle this has", replied his companion.

"Have you seen anyone pass here recently guys?"

"If it's your crazy drunk mate you are asking about then yes, he just staggered by five minutes ago. Look, pal, we tried calling the police, the track is fucked up ahead and he is probably going to kill himself. You best leave him and let the professionals deal with it mate."

"Thanks, guys", I replied. "I think the professionals might be closer than you think though."

In the distance, I could hear a dog barking and this one sounded real and alive. The animal had obviously got our scent, making the police change direction now that they realised the fugitives they sought were ahead rather than behind them.

"Tell the cops I have gone to try and find him, and we need help."

With that, I ran on and left the two bemused workers standing to look at each other in disbelief as they wondered what had happened to their usual lonely day in the woods.

It was hard to take in the scene that greeted me five hundred yards further on. In the midst of a mud-soaked landslide, I could see Harvey trapped in No Man's Land desperately clinging to the branch of one of the many fallen trees. How he had even got that far without sliding down into the loch was a miracle as he was clearly drunk to add to the mess he was in. He turned to look at me with the face of a cornered animal but then broke into a sad looking smile. "Fucked this one up Ralph, I was coming back but those fucking demons are in my head again, they were standing right where you are now mate. God, I am glad to see you, get your arse over here and get me out of this mess and bring the whisky with you, two bottles if you have them."

I started to edge with meticulous care over the mud and running water while trying to hold onto parts of fallen trees.

"Don't move an inch, Harvey, stay as still as possible and I will try to get over to you."

In the distance the sound of a baying dog could be heard, the police would no doubt be arriving at the two forestry workers who would be telling them the story of the crazy drunk and his friend.

"The police are just behind me Harvey, I don't know why or how they know, but I swear to God I did not tell anyone. You are a fucking big idiot, you could have handed yourself in this morning. Even this late on it would have looked so much better if you had given up voluntarily; why the fuck can you never do the right thing, just for once?"

He held out a hand while gripping the tree tightly with the other one.

"Jeez Ralph, well I'm glad it wasn't you, somehow the bastards were always going to get me in the end, probably the guy I gave my car too or some fucker who saw me driving that night. Anyway, what does it matter, I am done for now old boy. I might as well join the fucking corpses who are chasing me"

Suddenly I slipped in the mud and came crashing down into a mass of squelching wet dirt. Just as it looked as though I might be destined to slide towards certain death in the loch below I managed to grab desperately at a branch and cling on.

"Fucking Christ Harvey, everything you get me involved in ends up a fucking mess."

I scrambled back to my feet covered from head to toe in oozing mud and continued to edge my way too within a few feet of my companion. He was laughing although it was hard to tell if it was because of the state I was in or hysteria or drink, maybe all three.

"Give me your hand you fucking great lump", I shouted over the sound of the rushing water while trying to reach out.

As Harvey released one of his arms and held it out to me he gave a drunken smile,

211

"Promise me one thing Ralphy boy, promise me just one thing, tell me you will come visit me in prison because no one else fucking will."

But even before I could reply the smile was fading from his face as his eyes focused on the edge of the path I had just left.

I grabbed Harvey's hand just as I turned around to follow the gaze of his eyes. The old man and the boy both stood as if guarding any possible route back to the path. There could now be no doubt that walking death was upon us. The stench of rotting filth and mud pervaded every inch of our surroundings as the light dimmed to allow the eerie world of fallen trees and cascading water to blend in perfectly with the spirits that watched us. The path and the forest had waited in silence for this moment, patiently watching the meandering railway line to see if the two walkers had arrived yet. They had set the trap and from that point on there had only ever been one conclusion. I looked at the opposite bank more in desperation than hope but even if it had been possible to go that way it was now also blocked by the evil black dog that stood snarling and drooling as it started to slowly edge its way across the mud towards us. The scream of death rendered through the air as if carried on the wind to taunt us and make sure my companion knew that what he had done would never be forgiven. I held tightly onto Harvey's free hand and looked

212

into his eyes as he looked back at me and then we both finally understood why we had been thrown together. We both knew now that this moment had always been inevitable.

"You have to do it, Ralph, you know I am a fucking coward and will run forever, please, please do it for me......I forgive you.........please," his voice was pleading and almost hysterical as tears ran down ran from his eyes.

I smiled back at him as if to say goodbye and calmly whispered the words, "I am sorry too Harvey, really truly sorry it had to end like this. May God forgive us both, my friend." Then I reached over to the hand that grasped the branch to pull it free by the wrist. Leaning back into the tree allowed me to keep steady and grab the other arm, his body also held temporarily by the oozing mud. I held that position for the few seconds my strength would allow as we looked at each other. In that final moment of his life, we, at last, agreed that the captain's armband could be thrown into the mud. For the first time in our friendship we would be equal partners as both of us would now have blood on our hands. I gently let go of my grip and he slowly started to slide down into the filth, into the water and mud and then with sickening thuds his body gathered paced as it crashed into the broken trees to finally disappear over the edge. Silence for an eternity and then the scream that could have been a boy or a man facing certain death, followed by the splash as his body hit the water and then slowly disappeared into the black depths of the Loch.

Lost in the Ether

Entwined memories, long forgotten

Bottled and sent to the ether

An infinity of lost souls whose thoughts will float forever

Was it real, an opportunity lost, or a moment inconsequential?

An out of time bonding in a life full of rules

Now in the ether our memory lives while we are forgotten by all

More alive now than then could ever be

We are long gone but our entwined moment remains forever, lost in the ether.

## 10- I Miss You

The car pulled into the driveway and stopped. The man inside seemed to be caught in a trance as he sat staring at the large foreboding farmhouse. It had been gently decaying for years along with the surrounding garden, but now with its last full-time occupant gone the gradual decline had accelerated to the point where the building looked as though it had been empty for years rather than just three months. The summer growth had completely taken over what had once been a lawn with flower beds running up each side, now it was a mass of untamed confusion. Once cared for shrubs and bushes mingled with tall weeds and grass that overflowed and swirled in the warm wind that came down the valley. Gus stared at the dark imposing house through the car windscreen and just for a moment he considered restarting the engine and leaving the ghosts inside to go back to gently murmuring amongst themselves. It was as if the large black door was closed tight for a purpose, as though it was telling him he was not welcome back after all these years. *You never came when you were needed, you left us all to fade with the passing of time and then drown in our memories*, it seemed to whisper.

Gus thought back to that day almost forty years ago when he had walked out the door for the last time, still a young man in his mid-twenties finally ready to follow his older brother to the other side of the world. Of course, both he and Calum had been back to visit a few times over the years bringing the grandchildren and wives but it no longer felt like they belonged anymore. Once you had seen what the world was like outside the village it was impossible to return. The death of his father more than fifteen years ago had been the last visit despite all the well-meaning promises and good intentions. The fact was both Gus and Calum found Marian intimidating, someone they respected rather than loved. She had been a good mother, but the house had been run on her terms and none of the men would dare question anything she decided. Maybe it had been no coincidence that when the chance came the two boys had left one after the other to find a new life in Australia, almost as if they had to put as much distance as possible between them and their past. Gus remembered taking the loss of his father far harder than the recent passing of his mother but maybe that was because he was also nearing the twilight years of his life and the inevitability of death had less impact on him as each year passed. His mother felt like a distant stranger now, someone he thought he once knew. The person he had looked at in the hospital wired up to multiple clicking machines just seemed like some stranger he felt compelled to visit. Gus had been putting off going to the house for as long as possible because he knew that it held the real memories of his past far more than the barely breathing body of an old woman that he hardly recognized.

The truck entered Dalgowan and slowed to thirty miles an hour as Jacek looked for a sign that would show him the way to Duncraig farm. The journey from Carlisle had been easy enough but as usual, as soon as he hit the hills in Dumfrieshire his satnav started to lose its signal. Since moving from Poland a few years ago Jacek had driven his truck all over Southern Scotland, so he knew there would always be someone who could point him in the right direction. He pulled his lorry up outside a small convenience store and climbed down. Inside the store, a young man was tapping away on his mobile phone. "Hi, I am looking for Duncraig farm, any idea how I get to it?" For once the youth put his phone down and looked at the man.

"I don't think it is open as a bed and breakfast any more pal, the old lady who lived there died a week or two ago."

Jacek smiled before answering.

"No, it is ok mate, I am delivering a skip. They are going to clear everything in the house out, looks like it is going to be refurbished and sold on. It's a shame but they don't hang about these days, poor lady just in her coffin and the family has the place sold."

The young man nodded his head in polite agreement.

"Straight down the road towards Carlisle; Duncraig farm is the first turning on the right just after you leave the village.

He then went back to giving his six-hundred-pound handset the attention it probably deserved at that price, even if it still did not actually get a phone signal.

With an air of reluctance, Gus finally stepped out of the car and bracing himself walked slowly up towards the large door. A faded sign posted underneath the letterbox read, *Bed and Breakfast guests, please use the side entrance.* He turned the key in the door and felt it move stiffly against the pile of letters and newspapers jammed against it on the floor. The large wooden frame squealed in protest as it opened, and the probing rays of sunlight flooded into the damp unused hall for the first time in many years. At the very moment Gus stepped back into the house, Marian's spirit was at long last released to float out and melt away into the distant hills, while in the overgrown rear garden the last remnants of the bent scarecrow buckled and finally tumbled back into the soil. All that remained to welcome Gus back home was the damp rooms of the lifeless house and the black and white picture frames full of dead memories. In the distance, a lorry was already slowing up to take a right turn into the farm.

I knew the two detectives sitting opposite me could tell I was not giving them the full story. They kept repeating the same questions and would suddenly throw a new one in as if it was part of some pre-determined plan to catch me out. Mark did most of the talking and made the effort to seem friendly while his colleague Nerrisa would occasionally say something and then raise her eyebrows at my answer, like a silent assassin. "Tell me again why you decided to follow Mr. Lindean when he left on that last morning even though you say you had decided to hand him in?" said Mark.

"I told you, I just wanted Harvey to be the one who gave himself up, he wasn't a bad guy and I felt sorry for him", I replied.

"So how long was it that you and Mr. Lindean were such close friends, was it weeks, a couple of months maybe?" Nerrisa seemed to enjoy showing how clever she was by adding the answers into the end of her own questions.

"Well, you sound as though you know more about our friendship that I do so there is little point in me replying. Sorry, what was your name again Constable?"

Nerrisa's face flushed at the sharpness of my reply, but before she could attack again Mark jumped into referee.

"Mr. Casalles, it would help if you could just answer our questions. I understand you have had a traumatic time but try to remember that we are following up on the death of a child here."

I apologised but made sure I only looked at him as I spoke the words. The verbal jousting continued for most of the day, but I knew I had to stick to my story and leave out the parts that would have come across as either insane or at best trying to hide the truth. Any mention of spirits and rabid dogs would have led to more questions and possibly the accusation that I had a hand in the deaths of Harvey or even Maxime. They kept fishing for answers and it dawned on me that they suspected I might have known about my companion's involvement in the accident before we had even started our walk. I looked at the smug face of the assassin as she made another sharp comment and wanted to shout in her face, *you are looking at a fucking murderer Miss Marple, sat right in front of you and you can't even see it*. Of course, I said nothing and stuck to my story. The interview looked at long last to be winding down as Mark read over my statement.

"Is there anything you want to add Mr. Casalles, anything at all that you might have missed out?" the tone of his voice implied that it was more of a statement than a question. I could tell the assassin was about to play her trump card but replied anyway.

"No, I think I have told you everything I can remember." I watched in relief as Mark started to shuffle the papers of the statement together to imply he was finished with me. He turned to his colleague, "Nerrisa, have you any more questions?"

She continued to look straight at me, "Just one last thing you could maybe do for me Mr. Casalles, can you show me your left arm please."

I walked out of the police station in Stranraer a free man at last. I no longer cared what they thought; it just felt good to be alive after the events of the past few days. I would be re-interviewed by the team back in Norwich in a week or two as they remained unhappy about some parts of my story. The fact that I had forgotten to mention being attacked by a wild dog had given them the impression I was trying to hide something. So long as they could not implicate me in the death of Harvey, the worst that could happen would be a rap on the knuckles for not coming forward earlier to tell the authorities that I had known about my friend's involvement in the death of the little boy. The police had told me they had yet to recover Harvey's body from Loch Derry; it seemed he had simply disappeared into the mass of mud and trees that had fallen into the water after the landslide. I wondered if they would ever find him, somehow, I hoped not. The fact that his death would be put down to suicide at least gave him a little bit of respect. As though he finally had the courage to admit his guilt and accept the punishment. Ok maybe I had helped him along, but at least he had given me permission and in my eyes that counted as suicide. I booked into a rundown hotel for the night with a plan to catch the early morning train to Glasgow at eight o'clock. The phone stayed switched off, the next time I would speak to Meg would be face to face. I wanted her to see me walk up the street a changed man, ready to start over again if she would just give me the chance.

That evening I wandered around the quiet streets of Stranraer; the only places not closed for the night were either pubs or takeaways. That's the problem with stopping drinking, it's not just the booze you miss it's also the social side of sitting with fellow drinkers and losing yourself in alcohol-fueled conversation about everything and nothing. Well that's until the balance tips more to drink than social I suppose, because after that, your only interest is sitting by yourself and making sure the booze is always with you in constant supply. I entered what looked like a sports bar with those big TV screens hanging on every wall dishing out endless events no matter what time of day it is. At least this would give me something to do while I sipped my can of coke, I reckoned. Three young men sat at one end of the bar while an older man sat in the middle, all were supping away on frothy full pints of beer. They exchanged conversations at various points as the alcohol loosened their tongues and everyone felt the common bond of drinking together. I sat down at one of the tables feeling like an outsider and made an effort to watch a third-rate tennis match being played in a half-empty stadium in some European city, no doubt a warm-up for one of the real contests. Forty-five minutes later I was heading back to the hotel feeling more alone than I had ever felt in my life. It was strange to think I had left Chelmsford seeking solitude and isolation in the wilderness and now I missed Meg, I missed Harvey, I missed my kids, work, the shops, the streets, the crowds......... home. Yes, solitude without a drink was exactly that, isolation and loneliness. I desperately wanted to go home. That night I dreamed that Harvey stood before me, no longer haunted by the ghosts, no longer owned by his alcoholic demons and we shook hands as though he had forgiven me. Then his face gradually changed into mine and I was looking at my own image staring back at me.

The morning proved to be bright but with a sharp wind blowing from the Irish Sea into Loch Ryan. Stranraer had the look of a dead town now that the ferry terminal had moved down the road to Cairnryan just over six miles away. The train station sat perched on an embankment at the edge of the loch, a cold half a mile walk from the main street. I could see the empty space that had once been a busy ferry terminal that now separated the run-down train station from its potential source of revenue in the houses of Stranraer. Leaving the edge of the town to walk to the isolated station I passed a small group of people huddled in the Perspex shelter waiting for the far more conveniently placed bus service. The station itself had an overall cover reflecting back to the days when it had held the importance of being a terminus for trains to the south and boats from Ireland. Now it was overrun with seagulls perched on the iron supports of the roof and white bird droppings lay splattered along the edges of the platform and across the excess rusty lines of unused rail. The wind swept through the opening at the end of the covered station sending me into the small cold waiting room to seek some shelter. The only other human being in the station was the lady sitting behind the glass that separated the passengers from the token member of staff. It was good to see she had an electric fire to keep her warm while I almost froze to death.

"Good morning, God it's cold in here. I was hoping to go to London from Glasgow, but would it be possible to break the journey up and go via the Dumfries line and then take the Virgin train from Carlisle straight to London?" She looked at me and smiled,

"You could change at Ayr and miss out Glasgow altogether. That train would take you to Kilmarnock and you could then join the Dumfries line from there." I thanked the lady behind the glass for being so helpful and friendly. It always took me by surprise when railway staff tried to be polite; I suppose I expected them to be surly, the way they had been when I was growing before customer satisfaction graphs and team briefings became all the rage. Of course, her good mood might simply have been due to having a three-bar electric fire in her little office, maybe if it had only been a two bar she would have been a right misery and I would never have got to hear about the shortcut to the Dumfries line. Fifteen minutes later I heard the familiar sound of the approaching sprinter as it nudged into the little terminus to pick up the handful of frozen passengers waiting desperately to get inside the carriage for some warmth. Don't ask me why I had chosen to go through Dalgowan one last time rather than take the quicker train home from Glasgow. It was just something that I knew I had to do; maybe the path had not set me completely free just yet.

Four hours later I stood on the platform at Kilmarnock waiting for the little train to come in and take me to Dumfries and then onto Carlisle. Trains always seemed to make me doze off although now I was alcohol-free maybe the payback would mean I would struggle to sleep and eventually become one of those wide-awake baggy-eyed zombies who never get the chance to switch off from life occasionally. I set the alarm on my phone to wake me in an hour and a half just in case I slept through the Dalgowan stop. Almost as soon as the mostly empty train was in motion I felt the hazy thoughts drift over me, not quite dreams but that point in between where you are neither asleep or awake and your brain tries to keep order while sleep battles with it to scramble the order into confusion. I thought about Harvey and the ultimate price he had paid, not for killing Milo but for being an alcoholic. He was no more a murderer than I was, with both of us committing a crime through circumstance rather than design. The two of us had blood on our hands but at the exact moment of execution, neither of us had any choice. The chance to keep off the path that led to the forest had gone the very day we had lifted our first drink when barely teenagers. From that point on the trees had focused their gaze across the hills and waited for us to come home.

Carrie walked slowly towards the door; the self-confidence that usually surrounded her like a shield seemed slightly less formidable now. Maybe for once, she was questioning her own decision-making process and the first seeds of doubt had already taken root. At least she had walked out of her job rather than be dismissed but her petulant arrogance that day had come back to haunt her. New opportunities had not fallen at her feet as she had expected; the elephant in the room at every interview was always going to be: "Just one thing Miss Darnell, can you tell me why you left your last position at Calibar and Mitchell so suddenly. Why did you not even work your notice?" Keeping her head down as she walked past the smokers standing outside, Carrie pushed the door open and went through.

Feeling nervous at meetings had never been a problem before, she had always kept her emotions firmly under control; ready to drive the next project forward and challenge her colleagues to keep on track. Maybe that was the difference today, she was new, and the other attendees had no previous track record on which to measure her. Carrie moved her hand and placed it on her abdomen, maybe she could not feel anything moving yet but it did not matter, new life was growing and for the first time in years she smiled inside despite being sober. The eyes of the other people in the room looked at her in friendly anticipation as Carrie leaned forward in the seat. "My name is Carrie Darnell, and I think I might have a drinking problem."

She looked around the room and then suddenly her defences started to crumble, the outer shell of her armour collapsing to leave her exposed as though she was a little girl again.

"No... I am not being honest; my name is Carrie Darnell and yes... I do have a drinking problem." Then at last Carrie sat down and started to cry as helping hands moved in to comfort and finally welcome her back home again.

The buzzing of the phone alarm gave me a jolt and I looked up in panic at the electronic indicator attached above the door that separated the two carriages. For one confused moment, I thought I had slept through the Dalgowan stop but

I need not have worried. The moving dots on the sign read, NEXT STOP WILL BE DALGOWAN, THIS TRAIN IS FOR CARLISLE WHERE IT WILL TERMINATE. I could feel the brakes coming on and the carriages starting to slow for the village. A handful of people had joined the train since I had fallen asleep including a young mother with a boy in the seat opposite. They were getting ready to leave at the upcoming station and the woman was trying to keep her patience in front of the other passengers as she told her young son to stop playing on his phone or they would miss their stop. She gave me an exasperated smile as she staggered with bags in each hand to the door trying to nudge the boy forward in front of her. I turned my attention back to our approach to the station and looked on at the familiar view with a sense of anticipation. The window gave me a clear panorama of the familiar summit of Benrack and the distant green outline of the forest as it peered down at the small village. It had only been a week since we had set out from here, two alcoholics running from life as the pack closed in behind. One of us dead but hopefully forgiven; one of us alive and hoping for forgiveness. The train pulled up and stopped at the empty station while the guard opened the doors and stood on the platform to go through the motion of checking for any passengers. The young woman and the child hurried off the train and quickly disappeared down the side path to make their way into the village. Within seconds the guard was back inside and pressing the little buzzer to tell the driver that once again there would not be anybody leaving Dalgowan today. As the train started to slowly move out of the station I could see the figure that I had expected to be waiting for me, standing at the end of the platform. A large middle-aged man wearing a woolen walking hat and covered in wet hiking gear stood looking directly at me. The once white hair cascading down the side of his face now dirty and mud-stained. His eyes black and hollow without life, without humour, without tears, just motionless with death. We did not have to do anything, the fact we were both at the station at that exact time meant we understood each other. There would be no need for Harvey's ghost to follow me as I would know when the day came, that I was wanted back at the path. Then I alone would attempt to reach the end while knowing the end was waiting for me. It might be next week, or it might be in twenty years, but I would return at the appointed time to accept my sentence and join my friend in the dark depths of Loch Derry.

I Miss You

That first morning waking alone, only the ticking of the clock and me
I hear the raindrops, I feel the silence, I can touch the emptiness
I miss your laugh, I miss your warmth, I need your smile

Loneliness, Isolation, and silence
Tick tock tick tock so slow the hands of time that once moved so fast
I miss your hand, I miss your face, I want your heart beating next to mine

The whistle of the kettle, the ring of the phone, the knock at the door, no longer shared
Your shadow glimpsed in every corner
I miss your touch, I miss your whisper, I am lost without you

If only you could come back and let me live each second again
To let me hear your voice just one last time
To let you hear the words, I miss you.

# Epilogue

I bet you read the word epilogue and thought to yourself, how pretentious, who on earth does this dead guy think he is? Well look, if it makes you feel any better, I tend to agree. When I was younger I would avoid like the plague any books with the dreaded epilogue on the final few pages. Surely such a high brow summary at the end of a good story should only be reserved for classics such as, *To Kill a Mockingbird* or maybe *Pride and Prejudice*. I doubt I would even have been allowed to lace Ernest Hemingway's boots when I was alive so there is fuck all chance I would get the gig now I am a corpse. So, with that in mind, I thought it best to call the concluding part something like, *a last word from the dead*. The only trouble is I have already called this part the epilogue, so my next part is really the epilogue of the epilogue; anyway, hopefully, you get my point.

## A Last Word from the not so dearly departed.

I really do feel like a bit of a sponger asking if any of you could do me yet another little favour. First of all, can I say that the kind person who went and picked up the wet newspaper off the street in Chelmsford at the start of this tale is exempt. To make things easier, let us pretend her name was Brenda. I think we would all agree then that Brenda went way over and above the call of duty. Not only did she make the effort to at least start reading this tale, she also put on her shoes and walked down Moulsham Drive to look for the soggy old local rag with my obituary in it. Anyway, thanks, Brenda, now put your feet up and let us see if anyone else will be kind enough to help me out.

Actually, I have been thinking. I am probably being a bit presumptuous assuming that more than one person has read the story to this point; in fact, maybe even Brenda thought *fuck it* and gave up after chapter two. So why don't I just pretend someone is going to do this one last favour for me and describe what is required. I should also mention that there is a small reward at the end for the person who follows my instructions, but please try not to get too excited; it is not money or hidden treasure, unfortunately. Ok, that's everything cleared up then so here goes.

Firstly, you will need to check your appointment diary and find out if you have a spare day on the twenty-third of March; it can be any year, just so long as the date is right. Exact timing is a bit difficult, but I reckon if you aim to be at the rendezvous point say between two and five pm then hopefully things will work out. Now if you have read the story you will not be too surprised to find that the place you need to travel too is in that beautiful but remote part of Scotland known as Galloway. Unfortunately, I cannot give you the exact coordinates because that is a bit too scientific for me and of course it is no use using sat nav because there is fuck all chance of getting a phone signal where you are going to anyway. Now the actual place you need to find is the western end of Loch Derry and no matter how you play this, it is going to involve a good bit of walking. Trust me; you will be lucky to find a track around these parts never mind a road to take the family car along. I will just have to assume you can find your own way to the Loch and the rest should be easy. Now head along the Southern bank of the water for roughly half a mile and eventually, you should see an old wooden bench in front of you. I think it was put there many years ago maybe to give walkers a chance to rest and take in the spectacular view. Now the last thing you need to do is take a few steps back into the cover of the trees, maybe around two hundred yards from the bench. Any closer and you may spook the spooks and that would be a bit of a shame considering the effort you will have made to come this far.

So, let us assume you have followed my instructions to the letter and you are now waiting in anticipation while hiding unseen in the forest at the edge of the water. Do you see the two figures in the distance sitting on the rotting old seat? Even from this far you will be able to tell that they are two older gentlemen, maybe late fifties or early sixties. One of them is much taller than the other and is wearing a woolly hat, no doubt he is bald, but you will notice he has long white curls flowing out from under his bonnet. The other guy, the smaller one of the two is called Ralph. He has better hair and no hat but seems to be a bit uneasy, almost neurotic you might think. Personally, I reckon the smaller one is the better looking of the two, but then that's just a matter of personal taste I suppose. He is slimmer, that's a scientific fact even if you do think the taller one is slightly more handsome. Anyway, sorry I digress; let's get back to what I hope you will see. They will be huddled close together trying to keep warm and will pass a bottle of something back and forth to each other. The taller one will hog it a bit longer before handing it over, maybe that is why the smaller one is so neurotic. Now if by some miracle it is not hammering with rain and blowing a gale you might be able to pick up some snippets of their conversation and if you do this is what you will probably hear.

"This is definitely my last drink Harvey, I mean it this time. I am calling it a day, there has got to be more to death than drinking." The big guy with the hat will turn around and look at his friend for a few seconds before shaking his head and replying.

"Jesus Ralphie boy, will you never learn to chill out. I mean we are fucking dead and you still worry about drinking too much?" The big chap will then take a long hard drink from the bottle before continuing with his rant.

"Anyway, it is fucking typical of you Ralph, you kill me and then decide to top yourself right here in the middle of fucking nowhere. Of all the places in the world you could have dragged me to die, you pick this. Trees, water, and fucking none stop rain. Could you not have chosen to have your mid-life crisis in the Bahamas or at least Benidorm?"

The smaller one will then stare incredulously at the bobble-hatted one and reply rather sharply,

"Have you forgotten that you invited yourself on my fucking walk, I don't remember asking you to come in the first place. And another thing, if you had not cocked up everything in your life and mine as well, maybe we would not be dead in the first place and you could have gone to fucking Benidorm on your own." The smaller one then gives his big friend a ghostly nudge in the ribs before continuing. "Anyway, pass that whisky bottle over here before you finish the lot you greedy big bugger."

And of course, that's when the bobble-hatted one will smile before once again producing his trump card.

"No need to worry Ralphy boy, there is plenty where that came from. I have another two bottles of fucking scotch in my rucksack; that should last us until we get a real drink"

## Friendship

They say that when the storm blows in, hearts become heavy with the drift

Only then can a bond be made to join the flow, refusing to be cast aside like driftwood, circling your life as the current pulls you downstream

I have heard it said that the North wind gales can cast a shadow that will envelop the soul in an icy grip

Only then can a hand reach out to touch you from the depths, refusing to let you float alone towards the rage

I have always known that true friendship rides out the storm, seeking dry land despite the pull.

How many real friends do we meet in one life, accepting each other for what we are? How many will we ourselves stand beside to meet the tempest?